I0723632

BOOKS BY TINA FOLSOM

Ace on the Run (Code Name Stargate, Book 1)

Fox in plain Sight (Code Name Stargate, Book 2)

Yankee in the Wind (Code Name Stargate, Book 3)

Tiger on the Prowl (Code Name Stargate, Book 4)

Samson's Lovely Mortal (Scanguards Vampires, Book 1)

Amaury's Hellion (Scanguards Vampires, Book 2)

Gabriel's Mate (Scanguards Vampires, Book 3)

Yvette's Haven (Scanguards Vampires, Book 4)

Zane's Redemption (Scanguards Vampires, Book 5)

Quinn's Undying Rose (Scanguards Vampires, Book 6)

Oliver's Hunger (Scanguards Vampires, Book 7)

Thomas's Choice (Scanguards Vampires, Book 8)

Silent Bite (Scanguards Vampires, Book 8 1/2)

Cain's Identity (Scanguards Vampires, Book 9)

Luther's Return (Scanguards Vampires, Book 10)

Blake's Pursuit (Scanguards Vampires, Book 11)

Fateful Reunion (Scanguards Vampires, Book 11 1/2)

John's Yearning (Scanguards Vampires, Book 12)

Ryder's Storm (Scanguards Vampires, Book 13)

Damian's Conquest (Scanguards Vampires, Book 14)

Grayson's Challenge (Scanguards Vampires, Book 15)

Lover Uncloaked (Stealth Guardians, Book 1)

Master Unchained (Stealth Guardians, Book 2)

Warrior Unraveled (Stealth Guardians, Book 3)

Guardian Undone (Stealth Guardians, Book 4)

Immortal Unveiled (Stealth Guardians, Book 5)

Protector Unmatched (Stealth Guardians, Book 6)

Demon Unleashed (Stealth Guardians, Book 7)

A Touch of Greek (Out of Olympus, Book 1)

A Scent of Greek (Out of Olympus, Book 2)

A Taste of Greek (Out of Olympus, Book 3)

A Hush of Greek (Out of Olympus, Book 4)

Venice Vampyr (Novellas 1 – 4)

Teasing (The Hamptons Bachelor Club, Book 1)

Enticing (The Hamptons Bachelor Club, Book 2)

Beguiling (The Hamptons Bachelor Club, Book 3)

Scorching (The Hamptons Bachelor Club, Book 4)

Alluring (The Hamptons Bachelor Club, Book 5)

Sizzling (The Hamptons Bachelor Club, Book 6)

YANKEE IN THE WIND

CODE NAME STARGATE #3

TINA FOLSOM

1

———

Lilly Davis sighed heavily and pushed back a tear. She'd had no idea how rapidly Uncle Will had been deteriorating over the past two months since the death of his only son, Thomas Reed, at the age of thirty-seven. She'd been out of the country on a tour with *Doctors without Borders* in Central Africa, when she'd heard about her cousin's death, and had been unable to travel back to help her uncle get over his loss. A local outbreak of Ebola had forced the entire team of doctors and nurses to quarantine in a remote part of the Congo. Nobody had been allowed to fly, making it impossible for Lilly to attend Thomas's funeral. Nevertheless, she'd shed plenty of tears.

Thomas hadn't only been her cousin, but also her childhood friend. And even as adults they'd been very close, despite the fact that they'd seen each other less and less. Thomas had joined the military and been deployed to dangerous hotspots around the world, while Lilly had undergone rigorous medical training at the best hospitals and laboratories in the country, before specializing in infectious diseases and landing a job at a cutting-edge laboratory in Bethesda, less than ten miles from Washington D.C. Her department had asked for volunteers to accompany *Doctors without*

Borders to the Congo to assist them by testing for muted viruses in the region.

Lilly hadn't spoken to Thomas in the two months before his death, which wasn't unusual. Over the past three years, it had always been Thomas calling her, always from a different number. When she'd asked him about his location, he'd told her that he couldn't give her that information. She suspected that his deployments were top secret and hadn't pressed him. But she knew Thomas well enough to tell that he was stressed, and that whatever he was doing was taking a toll on him. More than once she'd told him that he'd served his country long enough, and maybe it was time to come home and get a less stressful job.

"Soon," Thomas had promised.

But it had never happened. And now, Lilly stood in Uncle Will's house in the outskirts of Washington D.C. surrounded by boxes with household items ready to be donated to charity.

"You look sad, Miss Davis," Deja Lashae said from behind her.

Lilly pivoted. Deja Lashae, a black woman in her late forties, looked at her. She'd been her uncle's home healthcare worker for the past year, until it had become clear that William Reed had to go into a home for Alzheimer's patients to get the care he needed. Deja was tall and looked fit and strong. Knowing that handling elderly patients involved a lot of lifting, Lilly realized that being a home healthcare nurse for an old man whose health was failing and who could be stubborn, required a physically strong person.

Lilly sighed. "I spent many happy hours in this house, visiting Uncle Will and Thomas. I can't believe Thomas is gone... and Uncle Will... it's sad to see him like this..." She and William Reed were now the only ones left of the Reed family. Her mother, Will's sister, had died a few years earlier of cancer, and her father had moved back to his native Canada after their divorce nearly twenty years earlier. Will's older brother had died in a car accident.

"That's what dementia does to people," Deja said with a

compassionate smile. "You lose your loved ones even though their body is still here."

"That's true, Deja. I should have come back earlier. Maybe I could have spent a little bit of time with him when he still had lucid moments."

"Don't blame yourself. Nobody could have guessed how fast the disease would ravish his brain after his son died. It was as if he just gave up after that."

"Were you with him, when he got the news of Thomas's death?"

"Yes, I was. Your uncle took it hard. It seemed like all life left his body right there and then." Deja let out a sigh. "And when Thomas's ashes arrived a few days later... oh, it was crushing."

"His ashes?" Lilly said with a start. "He was cremated?"

"Oh yes," Deja confirmed. "I would want to be cremated. Lots of people do it nowadays. It's cheaper too. You know, no casket, no large grave to maintain, and—"

"But Thomas didn't want to be cremated. I know it. So does Uncle Will. I've known it since we were kids. Ever since his mother died in a fire that broke out in a restaurant, he was horrified at the thought of being cremated." Lilly shook her head. "It was in his living will. Thomas made us all promise. He made me promise." Only Lilly hadn't even been in the country when Thomas had died.

Deja gave her a concerned look. "I'm sorry, Miss Davis, I don't know anything about that. And your uncle was in no condition to make any decisions. Besides, from what he was told when he got the news of Thomas's death, I got the impression that he had no choice about what happened to Thomas's remains."

Lilly furrowed her forehead. "What do you mean?"

She shrugged. "Something about an infectious disease and that it was in the interest of public health?"

"But that makes no sense. Did they say what he died of?"

Deja lifted her hands in a helpless gesture. "That's all I could get out of your uncle."

"I thought you were there with him when he got the news of Thomas's death."

"Oh, yes, I was, but your uncle called somebody after Thomas's ashes arrived. But I'm not sure what they told him. He said something about an infection risk, and that the government just did what they had to, but he was upset about it."

"Who did he speak to?"

"I don't know." Deja lowered her voice. "Just between you and me, I'm not even sure that your uncle spoke to anybody at all. Even in the months before his son's death, he came up with all kinds of stories that didn't bear much resemblance to reality. You know... conspiracy theories."

That surprised Lilly. Her uncle had never been one to indulge in conspiracies. He was a man of logic, of science, of facts. He'd been a mathematician at a university in his younger years. Later he'd switched to a career as an actuary working for a large insurance company. Clearly, her uncle was far from the person he'd once been, even though he'd greeted her joyfully when she'd visited him upon her return from the Congo.

"When I saw him last week, he seemed very clear."

"That's the thing with dementia," Deja explained. "One minute people sound as if they're perfectly fine, and the next, they don't even recognize you. It's a cruel disease."

"It is," Lilly said. Then she motioned to the boxes. "I'd better continue so I can get the house listed for sale. Thank you for helping out with this, Deja."

"Of course."

Lilly turned to continue with the next room, Thomas's old bedroom, while Deja returned to the kitchen, where she'd been cleaning out cabinets.

Thomas's bedroom hadn't changed much even though he hadn't lived there in over fifteen years. There was no carpet, just the old worn wooden floor that creaked in many places. The single bed he'd slept in as a teenager was still standing against one wall, the old wooden desk where he used to do his homework on the opposite one. There was a large bookcase with books reaching from algebra schoolbooks to Zen philosophy. The walls were adorned with posters of Bob Marley and Santana. Even when Lilly and Thomas had been teenagers, their taste in music had been considered retro.

For a moment, Lilly just stood there, letting the old memories of their childhood together draw her back to a time where everything had been simpler. Thomas had been somewhat of an odd kid. Too serious, too wise for his years, an old soul. But in a way, Lilly was so much like him, almost as if they were twins, not cousins. As twelve-year-olds they'd even developed their own secret code to send each other messages with secret passwords. It had been a game between them. A game for nerds.

Lilly pulled herself out of her memories. She had work to do. The real estate agent she'd talked to about listing Uncle Will's house had told her that she wanted to get the house painted and staged the following week, but that it was Lilly's responsibility to clear out all personal effects. A charity would come by the next day to pick up the furniture.

Lilly went through the books, tossing most of them into one of the boxes. There were none that she wanted to keep, none that meant anything to her. The closet still held some of Thomas's clothes that he had worn whenever he'd visited his father. The pants and shirts were out of fashion and worn. Thomas had never much cared about what he wore. Spending the majority of his adult life in uniform probably had something to do with that.

She tossed his clothes in another large box, then removed the old shoes and boots that lay on the floor in the closet. She was about to switch off the closet light, when something on the floor caught her attention. She crouched down to look at it more closely. There, in the corner where his old boots had stood, something was carved into the wood. At first, she couldn't tell what it was, but then she shone the cell phone light on it and recognized it. The few scratches that had most likely been made with a Swiss Army knife were meant to show the drawing of a flower, a lily.

Lilly sat back on her heels. She knew without a doubt that Thomas had carved the flower there. But when? If he had done it while they were still kids, he would have shown her. Softly, she knocked on the floorboard with the carving, then on the floorboard next to it. The sounds were different. The space beneath the flower sounded hollow.

She pulled her keys from her jeans pocket and stuck one of them between two floorboards. The floorboard with the flower lifted up easily, revealing a small hiding place not larger than a paperback. Inside lay only a few small items. She reached in and pulled them out.

The first item was a laminated ID card with Thomas's name and photo on it, which in itself wasn't surprising if it weren't for the organization that had issued it: the Central Intelligence Agency. Her heart stopped for a moment. Thomas had been a CIA agent? Was that why he'd never told her where he was deployed to? In fact, had he even been in the military, or had he lied to his family about being in the military when in reality he was a CIA agent?

Lilly set the ID aside, then looked at the two other items. One was a thumb drive, the other a black spiral notepad smaller than a cell phone. She opened it and realized that most pages had been torn out. Only a few pages remained. But they were blank. Why would Thomas hide a blank notepad? She shone her cell phone light on it to get a better look, when she noticed that the top sheet had indentations. Her heart beating like a jackhammer, Lilly jumped up and walked to the desk where she found a pencil. Placing the notepad on the desk, she brushed the pencil over the paper to reveal the writing that had left the indentations.

Henry Sheppard, CIA, 202-555-8978

But the lead from the pencil had revealed something else: a horizontal line crossing out the name and telephone number. Her heart beat into her throat. Was this a message for her? Was she supposed to contact Henry Sheppard? Or had Thomas crossed out the name and number because he'd changed his mind?

The longer Lilly thought about it, the less she understood. Had Thomas wanted to give her this message or not? She stood there for several minutes, contemplating what to do. But knowing that Thomas's remains had been cremated without his family's consent, she knew she had to make this call. Perhaps Henry Sheppard could shed light on what had happened to Thomas.

She dialed the number, and the call went straight to voicemail.

"You've reached Henry Sheppard. Please leave a message."

"This is Lilly Davis. I'm Thomas Reed's cousin. I need to talk to you about his death. Please call me. 202-555-6523."

She disconnected the call and heard a sound at the door to the room. She turned her head and saw Deja Lashae standing in the doorframe.

"Yes?" Lilly asked.

"I heard your voice and thought you'd called me. Didn't realize you were on the phone." Deja's gaze drifted past her to the closet. "You're making good progress I see. The kitchen cabinets are all empty now."

Lilly nodded, distracted. "Yeah, almost done here. Thanks."

2

J ack Porter looked at his cell phone again to verify that he hadn't made a mistake, but the address was correct. He stood in front of a large mansion in the outskirts of Washington D.C. The house was surrounded by a high wall on three sides, and a wrought iron fence on the side that faced the street. Lush vegetation dotted the large yard. He glanced at the sign affixed to the gate.

Sober Living Rehabilitation Center it said. *No soliciting.* Below it was an intercom system.

Jack instinctively touched the gun he wore in a holster under his jacket. If this was a trap, he'd be prepared. He pressed the button, and the intercom made a scratchy noise.

"Who are you here to see?" The voice was that of a woman.

"F—" He stopped himself just in time. The message to come to this address had presumably come from Fox, but he wasn't going to disclose his fellow ex-Stargate agent's code name. Instead, he said, "Nick Young."

"And your name is?"

"Jack Porter."

Though Fox knew him under his code name, Yankee. They'd met only a week earlier, when Fox had reached out to other Stargate agents via the Dark Web. Jack had made contact with him, suspicious at first that the person who'd been hunting the former Stargate agents might have set a trap. But it had become evident very quickly that Fox was the real deal—a precognitive like Jack.

A buzzing sound indicated that the gate was being unlocked. Jack pushed it open and stepped into the generous front yard. He headed for the wooden entrance door with the small portico meant to protect any visitors from rain or snow in the winter months and sun in the summer.

Without turning his head to either side, Jack scanned the area to his left and right, prepared to react if this was an ambush. But nobody approached him from either side. Instead, the door opened, and a pretty woman in her thirties greeted him.

"We've been expecting you, Mr. Porter," she said politely and ushered him inside.

He walked into the large entrance hall and gave the woman a once-over. She was casually dressed, but he wasn't sure whether she was unarmed or not. He couldn't see any weapon, but perhaps she'd concealed it cleverly under her belly, which made her look pregnant.

She smiled at him and pointed to the two armchairs in the foyer. "I'll get Nick for you. Please take a seat."

"Thanks," he said just as politely. "But I'd rather stand if you don't mind."

She left the entrance hall through a door to the right. When she was gone, Jack looked around. There was a desk with an old-fashioned phone as well as a few files on it that showed the colored tags a medical office used for their patient files. Jack walked closer. He flipped one of the files open. It contained only blank sheets of paper. Props. It confirmed that this wasn't a rehab facility for alcoholics or drug addicts. This was a front for something else.

Jack felt a tingling sensation at his nape, and instinctively his hand went to his weapon.

"I wouldn't do that if I were you."

Jack whirled around to the male voice addressing him. This

wasn't Nick Young. He'd never met the man pointing a gun at him, but he knew who he was, or rather *what*. The tingling sensation his presence had caused identified him as a precognitive. But that didn't mean Jack could trust him. After all, he suspected that it had been a precognitive who'd betrayed the top-secret CIA program he'd been part of. However, for some reason, there was something familiar about the guy.

"Where's Nick? What have you done with him?" Jack asked, eyeing him suspiciously.

"I'm right here."

Jack whipped his head toward the stairs and saw Nicholas "Fox" Young walk down from the second floor. He too held a gun in his hand.

"What's going on here?" Jack asked pointing at the stranger. "Who the fuck is he?"

"I could ask you the same thing," Fox replied.

"You know who I am! For fuck's sake, I helped you break into Langley only a week ago."

"Yeah, and maybe you had a reason for helping me, but you sure as shit ain't Yankee." Fox reached the first floor and now stood alongside the other man.

Jack looked the stranger up and down. Had they met before?

"I told you I'm Yankee, and that's the truth. I was part of Stargate, just like you." He tipped his chin toward the stranger. "And I'm assuming you're too. You're a precognitive, just like I am. I can sense it."

The stranger nodded. "You're right about that. But that doesn't mean you're a friendly. Or that you are who you say you are. You look nothing like Yankee."

Suddenly it clicked. "The list." He looked at Fox. "You looked at my photo on the list that you stole from the CIA."

Fox gave a quick nod. "Yeah, and turns out, you don't match Yankee's photo. Sure, you're his size, his hair color, eye color, you know, the usual stuff, and you're a precognitive, but you're not him."

"There's a reason why I don't look like the photo Henry Sheppard had of me."

"Of course there is," the stranger said sarcastically.

"I underwent plastic surgery to—"

"No wonder you're a pretty boy," the stranger interrupted, his tone revealing that he didn't believe a single word. "Why didn't we think of that?"

"It's true. You want to see the surgery scars?"

Fox and the stranger exchanged a look. "Wouldn't prove anything."

"Scott," Fox said to the man next to him, "how about running his face through the cranio-facial measurement program?"

"Scott?" Jack repeated, staring at the man next to Fox. "You wouldn't by any chance be Scott Thompson?"

Scott lifted his chin. "What's it to you?"

"I thought your mug looked familiar. Scott fucking Thompson! I think I owe you an ass-whooping for costing me first place in the cross-country survival test at the academy."

"And how would I have done that?"

"By lacing my gear with sugar water so a bunch of bees chased me. I had nine bee stings. Do you have any idea how much bee stings itch?" Jack growled.

Suddenly Scott smirked, then looked at Fox, while he put his gun back into his holster. "He's the real deal. Jack was a totally competitive asshole. He needed to be taken down a notch."

Jack walked closer to the two former CIA agents. Without warning, he landed a right hook under Scott's chin. "And you always thought you were better than the rest of us."

Scott rubbed his chin but didn't strike back. "Fair enough. It wasn't exactly my finest hour."

"Guess we're even," Jack said and offered his hand in greeting. "Nice to see that you survived."

Scott shook his hand. "Code name's Ace. Glad you did too. We need somebody with your competitive streak."

"Now that the introductions are out of the way, what am I doing at a rehab center?" Jack asked.

"This was Henry Sheppard's old house. Let me show you around," Ace said and put a hand on Jack's shoulder.

3

Ace and Fox led Jack through the house, the ground floor of which consisted of various offices and meeting rooms, storage rooms, and a large kitchen and dining room.

"Did you buy Sheppard's house?" Jack asked.

"Buy?" Ace said, shaking his head. "I inherited it. I grew up here."

For a moment, Jack let the news sink in. "So the rumors were true. You were the kid Sheppard adopted."

"Yes." There was pride and pain in his voice.

Ace hadn't only lost his mentor but also his father.

"Then there's one thing I don't get. How can you live here, just a stone's throw away from whoever betrayed the Stargate program and killed your father? How are you still alive?"

"With a little legal wrangling," Ace said. "I couldn't claim my inheritance after he was murdered. I'm sure they were waiting for me to come back here to kill me. I stayed away for three years. Before I came back here, I set up several shell corporations, all in foreign countries, and sold the property to one of them, then had that corporation sell it to the next, and so on, until it was impossible for anybody to follow the ownership trail."

"So you still own it, just not in your name," Jack said. "So why the rehab front?"

"I wanted to make sure that none of the neighbors got suspicious about the comings and goings here. For all the neighbors know, this is a very exclusive facility, and people entering the house at odd hours are thought to be celebrities wanting to guard their privacy."

Fox chimed in. "I've only been here a few days, but I'm impressed with the setup. And it works better than I thought it would when Ace first told me."

"When did all that happen?" Jack asked, addressing Fox. "A week ago you didn't have anybody but me to help you break into Langley. Why did Ace not help us?"

"I would have, had I known what hare-brained idea you guys came up with. Breaking into Langley!" Ace shook his head.

Jack jerked his thumb toward Fox. "Not my idea. This joker here thought it was a great idea."

"Hey, it worked," Fox said with a smirk.

"Could have just as well gone the other way," Jack said.

"Well, luckily it didn't," Ace said. "Because not only was I able to track down Fox because of it, we now also have a list of the former CIA agents involved in the Stargate program."

Ace opened the door to another room and ushered everybody inside. Jack stepped into the large computer room which seemed to be the nerve center of the building. There were no windows, and the walls had an odd shade of dark gray to them, but the room wasn't dark. Lots of bright lights illuminated the space.

Jack must have stared at the walls, because Fox said, "It's a special paint. It shields the room and its equipment from being eavesdropped on."

"Hey, guys."

Jack pivoted and saw the woman who'd let him into the house come up from under one of the computer consoles, a few computer cables in her hand.

"So, I guess that means the new guy is kosher?" she asked.

"Jack, meet Phoebe. She's my fiancée," Ace said.

Jack raised an eyebrow. He hadn't expected his fellow precognitive to have a private life. "Nice to meet you, Phoebe." Involuntarily, his gaze drifted to her belly again. Yes, she was definitely pregnant, though he had no idea how far along she was.

"You can stop staring now, Jack," Ace said from next to him.

Jack lifted his hands in a show of surrender. "Sorry if I stared, it's just... ahm... I'm surprised."

Phoebe chuckled. "Yeah, that makes two of us. And if we don't find the people who're coming after the Stargate agents in the next four months, I'm gonna have to give birth to this baby out of wedlock."

Jack cast a look at Ace but didn't say anything.

Ace held his gaze. "We can't exactly get married while people are after us. It's too risky. If anybody found the marriage license, they would have a way of tracking us."

"Makes sense," Jack said, even though he kept his mouth shut so as not to say what he really thought: that it was foolish to be in a serious relationship and bring a child into this world while being hunted by the people who killed Henry Sheppard and sent his agents running for their lives.

But he also knew that Fox was in a relationship too. And a serious one at that. Jack had met Michelle only a week earlier. "Is Michelle here too?"

Fox nodded. "Yeah. Where is she, Phoebe?"

"Somewhere in the attic. It's something about a line she has to run to bypass whatever... so that the servers run faster," Phoebe replied. "You know I don't speak tech."

"Somebody looking for me?"

Jack recognized Michelle's voice immediately. He looked over his shoulder and saw her enter the room. Her dark clothes were dusty, and there was a cobweb in her hair.

"Oh, hey, Yankee, you made it," she said, while Fox plucked the cobweb out of her hair. "Ew! The attic is so dusty. I hope that was the last time I had to go up there."

"I would've done it, if you'd told me," Fox said.

"Nah, it's not a problem. You had other things to do." She looked at Jack. "Is anybody hungry?"

Several replied in the affirmative.

"Okay, Phoebe and I will throw something together in the kitchen, and let you guys get on with it," Michelle said.

"Thanks, babe," Fox said.

When the two women left the room and shut the door behind them, Jack tipped his chin toward Ace and Fox. "So you guys all live here? Like in a commune?"

"Definitely not," Fox said.

"Only Phoebe and I live here," Ace replied. "On the second floor. But there are several guest rooms, in case Fox and Michelle can't go home for whatever reason. If you need a place to crash, you can stay here."

Jack shook his head. "I don't wanna cramp your style. I've got a secure place in D.C. It's not luxurious like here, but it's safe."

Ace motioned to a large desk, and they sat down around it. "Well then, let's figure out what to do next."

Meanwhile Fox pulled a laptop closer and logged in. Moments later, he'd pulled up a document and sent it to a larger screen on the wall.

Ace pointed to it. "This is the list Fox managed to get off the servers at Langley. These are the details on thirty-two Stargate agents. We can take several off the list: the three of us, as well as Zulu and Echo."

"Yeah, Echo is dead," Jack said with regret.

Fox nodded. "Yeah, you said he went bad? I filled Ace in on what you told me last week. And that he gave you the credentials for Sheppard's ghost login, which enabled me to steal this list."

"Unfortunately, that's all I've got on him. How did Zulu die?" Jack asked.

"Zulu's alive," Ace said. "He volunteered to go to the West Coast to find some of the men on this list. We're in contact, and he sends us regular updates on what he finds. He has leads on three agents that may be hiding somewhere in California and Oregon: Delta, Polo, and Whiskey."

Jack looked at the large screen. Each name had a colored dot next to it. "Red for dead? Green for the ones whose location you have?"

Fox nodded. "Yep. Blue for the ones Zulu has leads on."

"Assuming Zulu finds the three he's got leads on, that leaves twenty-four to find," Jack said. "Let's go through them. Perhaps I recognize some of them."

Ace cleared his throat. "Yeah, I'm afraid that my father made a mistake when he decided that the Stargate agents shouldn't know each other. But that doesn't mean that all of them are strangers to us. We all had to undergo regular CIA training." He pointed to Jack. "Just like you and I were at Camp Peary at the same time, others were too."

Fox nodded eagerly and scrolled through the list. "Ace and I already went through the list several times. The guys we recognized from either The Farm or other places, are marked in yellow. They will be easier to find, because we know them, we know their habits, and in some cases bits about their background and families."

"That still leaves a whole bunch of them," Jack said. He pointed to the top of the list. "Show them to me individually, photos and names."

Slowly, Fox scrolled through the list. Next to each photo was the real name and code name of the agent, as well as any special skills. Jack looked at each photo, let each name sink in, trying to recall any memories of the person.

"Next," he said, and every minute or two, he repeated the word.

"Not many left," Ace said, disappointment evident in his voice.

He couldn't blame the guy. Looking for somebody you knew nothing about, and who didn't want to be found, was worse than looking for a needle in a haystack. It was looking for a straw in a haystack.

Jack looked at the next photo and the name next to it.

Code Name: River

Name: Thomas Reed

He jumped up and pointed at the screen. "That's Thomas Reed. We were in the military together, before I joined the CIA. I had no idea Sheppard recruited him too."

"You knew him but didn't know he had the same gift as you?" Ace asked.

"I always felt the telltale tingling sensation at my nape when we were in the military together, but back then I didn't know what it meant. And Thomas and I never talked about our premonitions. I guess neither of us wanted to come across as weird or batshit crazy. But it does explain why he was able to get out of the line of fire so many times when we were fighting insurgents abroad. He always called it a sixth sense." He took a breath. "I know how to find him."

4

Wearing a white lab coat, Lilly sat behind her desk in her tiny office separated from the laboratory she ran at Delta Labs. She had four research assistants working for her, assisting with her current project to synthesize an anti-viral component for a new strain of a Kunjin virus that caused encephalitis. She was poring over the data on her computer, trying to figure out why the protein in the component wasn't stable enough to last longer than twenty-four hours, when her cell phone rang.

She glanced at the display. *Unknown caller*, it said. She answered it. "Hello?"

"Miss Davis? Miss Lilly Davis?" the man on the other end of the line asked.

"Yes, this is she."

If this was a sales call, she was ready to disconnect the call in an instant.

"This is Henry Sheppard. You left a voicemail for me."

Instantly, Lilly was fully focused on the call, her lab work forgotten. "Mr. Sheppard, thank you for calling me back. I wanted to talk to you about my cousin, Thomas Reed. I understand he worked for you?" At least that was her best guess. She lowered her voice, and added with a whisper, "For the CIA."

She glanced into the lab, but none of her assistants was close enough to the open office door to overhear her conversation.

"I can neither confirm nor deny your statement," Sheppard said evasively.

"I found his ID," she pressed on. "I have questions."

"What kind of questions?"

"How he died, and why he was cremated."

"I'm afraid that information is classified, Miss Davis."

"So he did work for the CIA?"

Sheppard cleared his throat. "I can't give you any information about Thomas Reed."

"Why not?"

"It's a matter of national security."

"At least tell me what he died of. I tried to find his death certificate, but it appears none was ever sent to his father. I need to see the death certificate."

"Miss Davis, I suggest you let this go. Your cousin is dead, and nothing good will come of you sticking your nose into government business."

"This is not government business. This is about my family. My cousin is dead, and he was cremated against his wishes. I think I'm owed an explanation."

There was a pause, and Lilly wondered if Sheppard had hung up on her.

"Mr. Sheppard?"

"Your cousin died during a training exercise. It was a tragic accident."

She needed to know more. "What happened?"

"The details are classified. I've already told you more than I should."

"And his death certificate? Do you have it?"

"I'm afraid that's outside of my area of responsibility. I'm sorry for your loss, Miss Davis. Have a good day."

He disconnected the call, before she could say anything else.

Frustrated, she tossed her cell phone on the desk. "Damn it!"

She wasn't satisfied with the answers Sheppard had given her. A training exercise? That could mean anything. Besides, it wasn't consistent with what Deja had mentioned—that an infectious disease might have been the cause. In either case, it didn't tell her how Thomas had died, and why he was cremated. She needed to find his death certificate. It would give her at least his cause of death, and also where he'd died.

Lilly did a quick Google search to find the information for the DC Vital Records Division. She called the number for records requests. A recording played.

"You have reached DC Vital Records Division. Your wait time is forty-five minutes. If you want to request a document, please visit our website at dchealth.dc.gov/vital-records and fill in the request form together with the applicable fee, proof of identity, and proof of relationship to the person whose record you are requesting. A copy of the record will be sent to you within four weeks. Thank you for contacting DC Vital Records Division."

Lilly disconnected the call. "Four weeks? Are you kidding me?" she ground out.

Not having a choice, she saved the link to the online form. She would fill it out after work and find whatever supporting documentation she needed to upload with it. She looked at the folder she'd put together. It contained everything she had on Thomas's death. She leafed through it once more, looking at everything with fresh eyes. There was a cremation certificate. She looked at it more closely. It was issued by a funeral home named *Peaceful Rest* not too far from the laboratory.

Lilly glanced at the clock. It was almost midday. She took off her lab coat and grabbed the file and her handbag. As she walked out of her office, she said to one of her lab technicians, "Andrew, I'm taking a long lunch."

Andrew looked up from his work. "See you later."

Outside, she walked across the small parking lot attached to the four-story building where Delta Labs was located and headed for the parking garage. She preferred parking in the five-story garage because it meant her car wouldn't feel like a sauna in the summer months. Lilly jumped in her car and drove to the funeral home. She parked in the large parking lot. There was no cemetery attached to the funeral home. She knew with certainty that the cemetery where Thomas's ashes had been laid to rest had a funeral home attached to it, even though she hadn't actually visited his grave yet. There hadn't been time since her return. So why had Thomas been cremated at *Peaceful Rest* and not at the funeral home associated with the cemetery where his ashes had been interred? Why not do everything at the same place?

Lilly entered the Victorian building that housed *Peaceful Rest* through the double door that led into a large foyer. To her left she saw a large room, where dozens of people dressed in dark colors were assembled. She spotted a coffin with flowers draped over it. Solemn music came from the room.

Lilly looked around, when a man in a dark suit approached her.

"Good afternoon, Ma'am, so sorry for your loss," he said and reached for her hand. "Please take a seat inside. We'll be starting in a moment."

"Uhm, I, uhm, I'm not here for the funeral," she said. "I wanted to speak to somebody in the office."

"Oh, my mistake," the man said quickly and pointed to a corridor. "The office is the last door on the right."

Lilly nodded a thanks, then followed the direction he'd indicated and found the office. She knocked and entered. A young woman sat behind a very clean and tidy desk, her attire subdued, her hair tied back, her make-up subtle.

"Hi," Lilly said. "I wonder whether you can help me."

The woman jumped up from her seat and walked around the desk. "Of course, Ma'am. I'm Caroline McDermott." She shook Lilly's hand. "Please do take a seat."

"Thank you, but it's just a quick inquiry," Lilly said. "My cousin was cremated here, and I wanted to get some more information about it."

She raised an eyebrow. "Oh? Was your family not satisfied with our services? If there's anything that was not—"

"No, no, that's not it," Lilly interrupted. "I just wanted to find out who requested the cremation. You see, I was out of the country when he died, and my uncle, uh, the father of the deceased has dementia... so..."

"No problem. What's your cousin's name?"

"Thomas Reed."

Ms. McDermott sat down behind her desk again and tapped something on her keyboard. A moment later, she looked at Lilly. "I'm sorry, Ma'am, but there's no record of a Thomas Reed being cremated here. Are you sure you have the right funeral home?"

"I'm certain." She dug into her handbag and pulled out the cremation certificate. "I found this in my uncle's papers to confirm that Thomas was cremated here."

"May I?"

Lilly handed her the certificate, and Ms. McDermott looked at it.

"Well, that's definitely our name, and the address is correct too, but"—she cast Lilly a regretful look—"this isn't even our stationary. The signature is wrong too. We never issued this certificate."

Stunned, Lilly stared at her. "Are you sure?"

"One hundred percent." Ms. McDermott pointed to the document. "This is a family business. There are only two people in this office who sign cremation certificates, and I'm one of them. The other is my father. This document is a fake. I'm sorry, Ma'am."

Speechless, Lilly nodded a thanks to Caroline McDermott and left the office. Why had somebody faked a cremation certificate? What would be the point? Something was fishy. What about Thomas's death was so important that somebody had to fake a cremation certificate?

What were they trying to hide?

5

———

To Jack's surprise, he found Thomas Reed's whereabouts two days after he'd met with Ace and Fox at Sheppard's old house. Jack stared at the plaque on the wall of urns at Shaded Pine Cemetery, a small cemetery in the outskirts of Washington D.C. Thomas was dead. Judging by the date of his death, Thomas had managed to hide from his enemies for over three years. They'd caught up with him two months ago.

Oh, Thomas, Jack thought, *why couldn't you hold out for another two months?*

Why had Thomas not been able to stay hidden? How had they finally caught up with him? Too many questions bounced around in Jack's mind as he looked at the stone behind which Thomas's ashes were held. Ashes... At the word a memory surfaced. Thomas had had a phobia stemming from his mother's death: fire. So why had he been cremated? It made no sense. They'd often talked about it when they were deployed to conflict zones around the world. Thomas had made him swear that should he be killed in action, he would be buried, not burned.

Was this a sign that something wasn't right? Had Thomas staged his death to get his enemies off his back? Had he meant to leave a message to his friends, to Jack in particular, by pretending he was cremated? It was odd to say the least, and worth investigating.

Jack knew exactly where to start: with Thomas's father. If anybody knew the truth about Thomas's death, it would be William Reed—if he was still alive.

An hour later, Jack found himself in front of an assisted living facility. He checked the address that he'd found online. No, there was no doubt: Will Reed now lived in an old folk's home. This too was a surprise. After all, Thomas's father, a fierce self-sufficient man, had sworn years ago that they would have to carry him out of his house in a box. What had made him agree to moving into an eldercare facility?

Jack entered the one-story building. Rather than feeling like a hospital, the interior had a cheerful, airy atmosphere. Soft music played in the foyer, and a reception desk that looked like it belonged in a spa was manned by a friendly young man.

"Welcome to Sunset Living, I'm Robbie. How may I help you?"

"Good morning," Jack said. "I'm here to visit an old family friend, Mr. William Reed."

"Ah yes, one of our new residents." Robbie smiled and pointed to a clipboard on the desk. "I'll have you sign in, and I'll need to see your ID."

Jack picked up the pen, and wrote a fake name on the form, then fished out the appropriate fake driver's license and handed it to the employee.

Robbie took a look at it, compared it to the name Jack had written down, and handed it back. "Here you go, Mr. Duke. I'll show you to Mr. Reed's suite."

"Thank you, I appreciate it."

Robbie stood up and motioned to one of the two corridors. Jack followed him.

"There'll be a mid-morning snack for the residents in a few minutes, and you're very welcome to join Mr. Reed for it."

"Thank you."

"He doesn't get many visitors, you know. You said you're an old family friend," Robbie fished, sounding just a little overeager to pump him for information.

But maybe Jack was just a little paranoid. Having lived in hiding for more than three years could do that to any man.

"Yeah, my father and Mr. Reed were friends," Jack lied.

"Oh, that's lovely. Maybe you can bring your father on your next visit."

Jack forced a friendly smile. "I'm afraid my old man died recently."

"I'm so sorry to hear that." Robbie stopped in front of a door. "Here we are." He knocked, then opened the door and stepped inside. "Mr. Reed, you have a visitor."

Jack entered the room behind Robbie.

"It's Mr. Duke for you," Robbie said.

Jack's eyes fell on the old man sitting in an armchair looking out the window as if he hadn't even heard them. He looked frail, his shoulders hunched forward, his arms slack on his lap.

"I don't know any Duke," Reed suddenly said.

Shit! Of course, Reed wouldn't know him under this fake name —or his new face. "Uh, still playing the old game of pretending not to know me."

Robbie looked at Jack and moved a step closer, and Jack was ready to do whatever was necessary should Robbie not believe him and cause problems.

"Some days he's better than others," Robbie said in a low voice. "But his dementia seems to get worse with each day."

"Dementia?"

"Oh, you didn't know? Yes, unfortunately, it's progressing at a really fast rate." Robbie pointed to Reed. "Just sit with him and talk to him. Many of our Alzheimer's patients seem to remember the distant past much better than what they had for breakfast. I'll leave you alone."

Jack nodded, and Robbie left the room and closed the door behind him.

Jack glanced around. The room was comfortably furnished with a bed, bedside table, a sofa with two armchairs, and a coffee table. There was a large built-in closet and a private bathroom. A few family pictures hung on the walls.

"Mr. Reed," Jack said and approached Thomas's father. "I'm Thomas's friend from the army."

Reed turned his head to glance at him. No recognition lit up in his eyes, and a moment later, he turned his head back to look out of the window.

"I'm Jack. Jack Porter."

"I knew a Jack once," Reed suddenly said. "I think... my brother... he was a soldier."

Jack sighed. He knew that Reed had had one brother and one sister. But his brother's name hadn't been John or Jack, but Michael. And he'd been a dentist, not a soldier. It was clear that Reed's dementia was quite advanced. Even if Thomas had staged his death and confided in his father, it was unlikely that Reed would be able to provide any information about it.

Maybe if Jack played along, he could trigger some memories in the old man. "Yes, your brother. Remember me? I came back from fighting a war."

A smile spread on Reed's face. "The steak was burned. You left it on the fire too long."

"At the last BBQ, right?" Jack said. There was a kernel of truth in the words Reed had spoken. At the Reed family BBQ Jack had been invited to just before he'd joined the CIA, there had been a little incident while Jack had manned the grill.

"I was supposed to watch that the flames weren't going too high." But he'd been distracted by a beautiful girl who'd arrived. He'd recognized her immediately, although he'd never met her before. Thomas had shared many pictures and stories while on deployment making Jack feel like he already knew her. "Your niece was there."

"Niece?" It seemed as if he didn't understand the word.

"Lilly," Jack helped.

"Lilly. A beautiful flower. My garden... all the flowers are blooming."

Jack swallowed down his disappointment. Reed wouldn't be able to tell him anything useful. It was sad to see him like this. No wonder he was living in an assisted living facility now. He couldn't live alone any longer. He needed full-time care.

Still, Jack had to give it one more try.

"Thomas is gone. Do you know where he went?"

Suddenly Reed turned his head toward Jack and locked eyes with him. "Thomas?" A tear rolled down one cheek. "They got him."

"Who?"

"They always get them in the end. They're everywhere." Reed's eyes shot to the door. "Even here. They're here in my house... I should have known... He shouldn't have come."

"Thomas? Thomas shouldn't have come?"

"She lied to me. It was her."

"Who? Who lied to you?"

"I have to warn his friends. They're coming for all of them."

"Thomas's friends? You have to warn Thomas's friends?"

"Who are you?"

"I'm Jack. I'm Thomas's friend."

Reed shook his head. "The government sent you. The government sent her. They tricked me. And Thomas paid for it. They found him because of me."

He suddenly started rocking forward in his chair, visibly distraught. Jack reached for his hand and squeezed it.

"I'm sorry, Mr. Reed. I'm sorry that Thomas is gone." Despite the incoherent things Reed was saying, his emotions were genuine, and they hinted at the truth: that Thomas was really dead.

"It's my fault." He reached for a photo that stood on the windowsill. "My fault."

Jack looked at the photo. It had been taken on the day of the BBQ, almost seven years ago. The photo pictured Reed, his son Thomas, his niece Lilly, and another man whose name Jack couldn't remember. The morning after that picture had been taken, Jack had received news to report to the CIA immediately. Henry Sheppard had made him an offer to join his top-secret Stargate program, but it had come with a condition: to leave his previous life behind and cut all ties with friends and family immediately.

Jack now focused his eyes on Lilly in the photo. She'd been the only thing he'd regretted leaving behind, because the night they'd spent in each other's arms after the BBQ, had ignited a need in him that he'd never been able to satisfy. The need to make Lilly his. But all they'd had was one night.

He shook his head. He wasn't one for daydreaming. He didn't have that luxury.

"Mr. Reed, I—"

Jack didn't finish the sentence. In fact, he didn't even know what he'd wanted to say to Reed, because suddenly everything blurred around him. A scene played out in front of his eyes. He knew what it was: a premonition. He had the gift of foresight, just like his fellow Stargate agents. It was the very reason why he and the other precognitive agents were being hunted.

He recognized Lilly immediately. She hadn't changed much in the seven years since their night together. If anything, she'd grown more beautiful. Her blond hair was the color of wheat. She wore it a little shorter now than seven years ago, but it still touched her shoulders, the soft curls framing her delicate face. Her lips were of a rich red, though he could tell that she wasn't wearing lipstick. Her eyes were still the same light grey accentuated by long lashes.

Lilly wore a white coat, the kind medical personnel wore. When he'd met her, she'd already been in her third year of residency at Johns Hopkins Hospital in Baltimore. Thomas had been so proud of her. Jack concentrated on the vision playing out in front of his inner eye. Lilly walked across a courtyard to a food truck. She ordered food and paid for it, then moved to the side and sat down on a bench, while waiting for her order to be prepared. Jack was able to read the name on the truck: *Jose's Enormes Tacos*. At the truck, more medical personnel stood in line to place their orders. Meanwhile, Lilly's cell phone rang, and she fished it out of her handbag and answered it.

"Hello?" She paused for a moment. Then she said again, "Hello?" A few seconds later she shrugged and put the phone back into her bag.

A few moments passed until somebody from the food truck called out Lilly's name. "Lilly, three beef tacos."

Lilly jumped up and walked toward the truck. That's when Jack saw it: a red dot on Lilly's forehead. There was no sound when the bullet struck. Lilly collapsed on the spot. Jack tried to force the vision to show him where the sniper had been hiding, but the scene before his eyes was already blurring.

A moment later, he was looking at Reed again. The old man stared at him. "Thomas, son?"

"I love you, Dad," Jack replied, knowing the old man needed to hear the words even though he wasn't Thomas. "I have to go."

"Don't let them win."

He wouldn't. Because now things had gotten even more personal. Lilly was in danger, and Jack would move heaven and earth to save her from the unknown assassin.

6

———————

Lilly stood in her office and looked out of the window to the plaza below. There were a couple of food trucks that had arrived around ten a.m., preparing for the lunch crowd. There were plenty of benches and trees to provide shade for the many office and lab workers who liked to enjoy their lunch al fresco. Delta Labs had also commissioned several pieces of art from local sculptors to make the area look less sterile, less like another dull office park at the outskirts of Bethesda.

Lilly had left several more messages for Henry Sheppard from the CIA after her visit to the funeral home two days earlier. He still hadn't called her back. But she wouldn't give up so easily. She picked up her cell phone and redialed Sheppard's number. Again, she only reached his voicemail.

"Mr. Sheppard. This is Lilly Davis again. Like I said yesterday, and the day before, the cremation certificate for Thomas Reed was a fake. The funeral home confirmed it. I find this highly suspicious, and since you seem to be the only person who has information about my cousin's death, I need to talk to you. Something isn't right, or why would somebody forge the paperwork? You have my number."

She disconnected the call. A moment later, her cell phone rang. "Yes?"

"This is Peter Lancaster from Shaded Pine Cemetery. Am I speaking to Ms. Davis?" the man at the other end of the line said.

"Yes, thank you for calling back." The previous afternoon she'd left a message at the cemetery where Thomas had been buried.

"No problem. I looked into your query about your cousin, Thomas Reed. I'm afraid there isn't much. He was cremated at a different facility, and the ashes and the cremation certificate were transferred to us."

"Do you know who sent the ashes to you?"

"Hmm. The document for transfer was signed by William Reed. I believe that's the father of the deceased."

"Are you sure?"

"Yes. He was also the one who purchased the space in our urn wall and the annual maintenance plan."

"In person?"

"I'm not sure. Many of our older customers call rather than visit us personally, you know. But the document was signed by Mr. Reed."

"Could you perhaps text me a photo of the document?"

"Of course. I'll send it over in a minute. Is there anything else you need?"

"No, thank you very much."

A few seconds after she disconnected the call, her phone chimed, announcing the arrival of a text message. She clicked on the photo and zoomed in so she could read the signature. At first glance, it looked like her uncle's but she knew it couldn't be his. A year ago, Will Reed's hands had started to tremble, and the doctors believed that he was developing Parkinson's. Her uncle could have never signed the document in such a neat way. His shaking hands would have prevented it. Somebody had forged his signature, and judging by the striking similarity to his signature before he'd developed Parkinson's, Lilly guessed that somebody had copied it from another legitimate document and pasted it onto the one Shaded Pine Cemetery had received.

She was at a dead end. Without the death certificate she couldn't investigate further. DC Vital Records Division had sent her an automated email confirming that they'd received her request for Thomas's death certificate, but it was anybody's guess how long it would take before she received it.

The USB stick she'd found in Thomas' room had been of no help either. It contained no data.

Lilly stared out of the window. Due to Delta Labs' location far from downtown Bethesda there were pitifully few choices when it came to restaurants. In the plaza below, it was getting busy. Lilly's stomach growled involuntarily. Time to take a break and eat something before the line at the only two food trucks grew too long. A taco from the popular taco truck in the plaza was just what she needed now.

She grabbed her handbag, shoved her cell phone into it and walked through the lab.

"Going down to grab lunch," she announced to the lab staff. "Does anybody want anything from the taco truck?"

Several 'noes' echoed in the lab.

"Andrew? How about you?" she asked, since he hadn't replied.

He looked up from his work. "No, thanks, Lilly, I'm fasting today."

"Good for you," Lilly said and headed outside.

Instead of taking the elevator down, Lilly opted for the stairs. She needed a little exercise. She was still getting over the news that her cousin had been a CIA agent. And there she'd thought he was in the military, fighting foreign wars for his country. In truth, he'd served his country in a different way. Why had he never told her what he really did? After all, they'd been so close.

"What can I get you?" the guy in the taco truck asked.

Lilly hadn't even looked at the menu posted on the outside of the truck. She always ordered the same. "Three beef tacos."

"Name?"

"Lilly."

She handed him her credit card, and he swiped it, then made her sign the receipt. She stepped aside to let the person behind her order. A few yards away was an empty bench. A short distance behind it stood a large sculpture made of different colored glass. It depicted a heart.

Lilly walked to the bench and sat down. She allowed the rays of sunshine to kiss her face and took a deep breath. Her mind went back to Thomas. She still couldn't believe that he'd been a CIA agent. And clearly a good one, because not even she had suspected that he kept a secret from her. What exactly had he done in the CIA?

The ringing of her cell phone pulled her out of her thoughts. She looked at the display, but it only said *Unknown Caller*. Was Henry Sheppard finally calling her back?

"Hello?"

There was static in the line, a garbled voice, but she couldn't understand what the person said.

"Hello?" she repeated, but the static in the line was getting worse.

She shrugged, and disconnected the call, before putting the cell phone back in her handbag.

Just then, somebody from the food truck called out her name. "Lilly, three beef tacos."

7

———

"Fuck!" Jack cursed, while jumping out of the car.

He'd figured out where Lilly's would-be assassination would take place by calling the number for *Jose's Enormes Tacos* and asking them where their truck was parked today. He'd raced there breaking all kinds of traffic laws, unsure what time the event would take place, although judging by the lunch crowd in his premonition it would be around midday.

While in the car, he'd tried Lilly's cell phone number, the one she'd given him seven years earlier. It was still in service, but it had gone straight to voicemail. He hadn't bothered leaving a message, because if he didn't reach Lilly in time, she'd never get it. He continued calling her, until he finally got through.

He heard a voice, but the static in the line prevented him from being able to understand what Lilly said.

"Lilly, run back into the building!" he warned her, hoping that she could hear him over the static. "Somebody is trying to shoot you."

"Hello?" he heard through the static, confirming that she hadn't heard him.

"Shit, shit, shit!"

Jack already spotted Lilly sitting on the bench and sprinted toward her. Just a few more yards. He nearly collided with a teenager listening to something on his earphones but avoided him at the last second. Jack raced past him, then saw in horror that Lilly stood up from the bench. Somebody from the taco truck had called her name. He only had seconds now.

Jack was three yards away from her, when he saw the red dot on her forehead. His heart stopped, but his body didn't. He lunged toward her, tackling her to the ground, when he heard the sound of something hitting glass and breaking it. He glanced up. The bullet had struck a glass sculpture several yards past the bench.

"Active shooter!" Jack yelled out to the people milling about the plaza.

The shattering of the glass sculpture had alerted everybody, and people screamed and ran for cover. Beneath him, Lilly groaned.

"We've gotta get out of here," Jack said, lifting himself off Lilly, while he glanced back. Since the bullet had hit the sculpture behind the bench, it was easy to guess where the assassin was shooting from. "Stay low."

Lilly seemed dazed, but he didn't have time to check if the fall had injured her, because the shooter was still up there somewhere in the parking garage, aiming at them. Jack grabbed Lilly and pulled her with him, when another shot rang out, but Jack had already pushed Lilly behind the taco truck and out of the line of fire. Behind it, he took a breath and ran his eyes over Lilly. She looked disheveled, and her knees were bruised, but other than that she seemed unhurt.

"Oh my God! What's happening?" Lilly asked, her breathing choppy, her voice laced with panic.

"I'm gonna get you outta here. Take off your lab coat."

"Why?" She cast him a confused look.

He motioned to where he'd parked his car. "We've gotta run to safety. And without your lab coat the shooter won't immediately recognize you." He was already tugging on her coat and helping her out of it. He took her arm and pulled her up behind the safety of the taco truck.

"My handbag," she said and reached down to the ground.

Jack grabbed it and handed it to her. Then he looked in the direction of his car, making himself familiar with anything that could provide cover: a few smaller trees, trashcans, and a few cars.

"My car is the red Toyota." He pointed to it. "Do you see it?"

"Yes."

"We need to run there as fast as we can."

Lots of people were already running away from the plaza, screaming. He hoped that the chaos in the plaza made it harder for the shooter to find his target.

"Ready?"

She nodded.

Holding Lilly's hand, he took off running, taking advantage of the trees between the taco truck and his car. A few yards away from where he'd stopped the car, he gave Lilly another instruction.

"Get in on the passenger side. The door is unlocked. Then duck."

She didn't say another word, but continued running. Jack let go of her hand and ran toward the driver's side. From the corner of his eye, he saw Lilly sprint toward the passenger side door and rip it open.

Jack reached the driver's side, and by the time he was inside the car, Lilly had already slammed the passenger door shut and was ducking down in her seat. Jack started the car and put it in reverse.

"Hold on to something."

Lilly braced herself on the dashboard, her head between her legs, while Jack did a three-way turn so fast the tires were smoking. Seconds later, he was in the street barely avoiding a crash with a taxi as he drove down the wrong direction on the one-way street. But he didn't care. They had to put enough distance between them and the shooter, before he could worry about anything else.

But first he had to make sure nobody could track them. "Do you have your phone?"

"Yes."

"Give it to me."

She dug her phone out of her handbag. "Should I call 9-1-1?"

"No, hand it to me."

She handed it to him, and he tossed it out of the car.

"What the hell?" she cursed. "Why did you do that?"

"So we can't be tracked."

At the next side street, he turned. This wasn't a one-way street, and finally, he could take a breath. He gave her a sideways glance.

"Lilly? Are you alright?" he asked again, orienting himself to find the best route to take them to a safe place.

Stunned, she stared at him. "Who are you, and how do you know my name?"

"I'm Jack. Jack Porter. I was Thomas's friend."

"Jack?"

From the corner of his eye, he noticed that she shook her head.

"I knew Jack Porter. And you're not him. Stop the car and let me out."

"I can't do that."

8

———

L illy's heart beat into her throat. She'd been kidnapped!

She was still panicked about the shooting in the plaza. She would have gotten killed if it hadn't been for the man who'd pushed her out of the line of fire. That much she believed. But had it all been staged, the shooting, the panic at the plaza, so he could abduct her without her putting up a fight? And the gall of the man to claim he was Thomas's friend Jack Porter! As if she didn't know what Jack looked like!

"Stop the car now! Or I'll mace you!" she bluffed and reached into her handbag.

"If you really had mace on you, you would have already used it. Nice try though," he said.

Was that a smirk on his face? How dare he!

Clearly the man wasn't easily fooled. She glanced outside, gaging the speed of the car.

"I wouldn't do that. You could get hurt."

"Do what?" she spat.

"Try and jump out of the moving car." He gave her a sideways glance and pointed to her legs. "You've already got bruises on your legs from earlier."

She looked at her knees, and only now saw the abrasions and the blood on them. She hadn't even felt the pain until now, too much adrenaline pumping through her.

"Why are you doing this? What do you want? A ransom? I have to disappoint you. I've got a mountain of student loans, and no savings."

"If I'd left you back there at the plaza, you'd be dead now."

"Can't you at least slow down?" she asked. She pointed through the windshield. "That light's already yellow."

But he raced through the next intersection with the light turning red, killing her hope that she could escape while the car was waiting at a red light.

"Lilly, take a breath. I've gotta get us to a safe place before they can catch up with us."

"Catch up? The shooter is back there at the plaza. You make it sound like I was the only target. I heard several shots."

He looked at her, and for the first time she noticed the deep blue of his eyes. Jack had had eyes like that. They'd drawn her to him that day at the Reed family BBQ.

"Yes, and had the first one hit you, there wouldn't have been any others. It was a sniper, and he had you in the crosshairs. I saw the laser on your forehead."

"That's ludicrous." Though the knowledge that somebody had aimed at her made her shiver. "No... no... why would..." Then the events of the last few days sank in. What if it had something to do with Thomas's death?

"Who are you really?" she finally asked and looked at him again. Had Henry Sheppard sent him?

He was handsome. She had to give him that. Tall, muscular, with dark blond hair, a straight nose and high cheekbones, a strong chin. Not a single ounce of fat on his frame.

"Like I said, I'm Jack Porter." He suddenly unleashed a smile on her. "And you've grown even more beautiful in the last seven years."

Her heart skipped a beat. Seven years. That's how long it had been since she'd seen the real Jack Porter, the man in whose arms she'd spent a passionate night, only to wake up alone.

"If you knew what Jack Porter did, you wouldn't claim to be him."

He didn't respond. Instead, he took a few more hasty turns until he finally drove into an underground garage. There, he had to drive slower, and she eyed the handle of the car door again. The moment he slowed the car as he drove around a bend, she pulled on the handle.

Nothing happened. The door didn't open. She spun her head toward him.

"You, you..."

"It's for your own good," he claimed.

A few seconds later, he pulled into an empty parking spot and jumped out of the car. He ran around the car and opened the passenger side door for her and pulled her out.

He didn't let go of her arm.

"Please let me go," she begged now. "I won't go to the police. I won't tell anybody about you kidnapping me."

But he dragged her to another vehicle, a white van. "I'll explain everything when we're at the safe house. I promise you, Lilly."

Then he opened the side door of the van and forced her inside. It was dark inside.

"Sit on the bench. And put the seatbelt on."

Then he closed the door, and she had no choice but to follow his order.

Moments later, they were back on the streets again, though Lilly couldn't see where they were heading. There was no window in the back of the van, and the separation between the driver's cabin and the back only had a tiny window that allowed her to see the back of her kidnapper's head.

She slumped back on the bench, and a tiny sob tore loose from her throat.

What would happen to her now? Would he rape and kill her? Dump her body in a ditch? Why? Why was this happening to her?

She didn't know how long they were driving, until the van finally stopped. Her abductor killed the engine. When the door to her prison opened, light streamed in. A hand reached for her.

"Lilly, come out, we're here."

She allowed him to help her out of the van and looked around. They were in a garage.

He closed the van door behind her and ushered her to a door. It led into a house.

"We're safe here for now," he said and closed the door to the garage behind them.

Lilly walked farther into the house. There was a small living room, a kitchen with a dining area, and two other doors that were closed. She assumed one was a bedroom, the other a bathroom.

"Take a seat," he said and pointed to the couch. "I'll get a first aid kit."

To her surprise, he left her alone in the living room and opened one of the other doors, which she'd rightly assumed was a bathroom. She heard him open and close cabinets and used the time to look around. There wasn't much decoration in the small one-story house. As if nobody really lived here. She'd seen vacation rentals that had more character than this house.

To get to the front door she would have to pass by the open bathroom door. Treading softly so as not to make a sound, she stalked toward it, but she didn't reach it. Jack stepped out of the bathroom, blocking her escape route.

He tilted his head a little to the side. "Please." He motioned for her to return to the living room. He set the first aid kit on the coffee table.

"I'm sorry that I had to push you so hard," he said in a soft tone, "but a second later, and you would have had a bullet in your head. I wish I could have gotten there earlier, but the traffic..." He sighed and ran a hand through his hair. A shaking hand.

That surprised her. Why was his hand suddenly shaking? And something else in his statement didn't make sense.

"Are you saying you knew about the shooting in advance?"

He met her eyes, and for a few seconds he said nothing. "First things first." He pointed to her knees. "Let's get you patched up." He took a step toward her.

"No!" She surprised herself with the firmness in her voice. "First you tell me who you really are."

"Fair enough." He sat down on the armchair and pointed to the sofa. "You might want to sit down for this."

Reluctantly, she sat down on the sofa.

"I am Jack Porter, and I was in the military with Thomas Reed, your cousin. And the reason you don't recognize me is because I had plastic surgery."

She huffed. "Yeah, right! What baloney! You're not Jack. I know Jack. I slept with Jack, so trust me when I tell you that I would recognize him. Sure, you're the same height, the same build, and even the same eyes, but that's where all similarities end, so don't think you can con me into believing you're him."

A slow smile spread over his face. "I get it. How much do you remember of that night seven years ago?"

"Everything!" It was true. She'd relived every second of her night with Jack many times over.

"Good. Then I guess you'll remember this." He stood up and put his hand on his jeans. He opened the button.

She jumped up, ready to flee. "What the fuck are you doing?"

"Showing you proof that I'm Jack."

He lowered the zipper and pushed his jeans down to mid-thigh. Then he hooked his thumbs into the waistband of his boxer briefs and pushed them down too.

His cock jutted out, heavy but relaxed. She couldn't rip her gaze from the sight. There was the proof.

"Your birthmark."

Right there on his cock was a birthmark that looked like the state of Texas. She'd seen it the night of the Reed family BBQ, after she'd gone back to Jack's hotel where they'd made love all night. It wasn't something that could be faked, or that many people even knew about.

She took a step toward him, but there was no doubt in her mind. This was Jack. The man who'd broken her heart.

"Believe me now?" he asked.

She lifted her head. "Yes, I believe you."

Then she balled her right hand into a fist and punched him in the face as hard as she could.

His head whipped to the side, and he groaned.

"Guess I had that coming for a long while."

9

———

Lilly had taken him by surprise. It shouldn't have. After all, he'd left her without a word or an explanation the morning after their night of lovemaking. Like a thief in the night, he'd disappeared. He hadn't been able to tell her the reason why.

"For what it's worth, I'm sorry about what happened back then," he said while he pulled up his boxer briefs and pants and zipped up.

"Well, thanks a lot. That's exactly what a girl wants to hear when a guy disappears after he's gotten what he wanted."

"I never got what I wanted." The words were out before he could stop them. They were the truth, although he hadn't wanted to admit this to her.

"Now you're insulting me by insinuating that I'm not good in bed?"

She'd totally misunderstood him.

Lilly balled her hand into a fist once more, but Jack grabbed it before she could punch him again and held it tightly. One punch was enough.

"That's not what I meant by it." He should keep his mouth shut and not take her bait, but he hated lying to her, hated pretending that the night seven years ago had meant nothing.

"Oh please!" she scoffed.

"I wanted you, but I couldn't stay. I had to leave you…"

She pulled up her lip in a sneer. "Let me guess: you're a secret agent like Thomas."

At the words, he let go of her fist and reared back. He hadn't been prepared for this. Had Thomas told her that they'd both been recruited into the CIA? Had Thomas known that Jack had been in the same program? Oddly enough, Jack hadn't known until two days ago when he'd recognized Thomas's picture on the list of Stargate agents. Clearly, Henry Sheppard had made Thomas the same offer, and given him the same condition: not to tell anyone. Not to share their secret.

Lilly locked eyes with him. "Oh my God, it's true. You're in the CIA just like Thomas."

He let out a breath, weighing up whether it was wise to tell her the truth. He hesitated.

"Don't lie to me, or I'm walking right out that door, and you'll never see me again," she warned, and he knew she meant it. From all the things Thomas had told him about her over the years, he knew she was serious. She didn't take crap from anybody.

"All right, you want the truth. Yes, Thomas and I were in the CIA."

"Were?"

Jack nodded. "Our program was eliminated." It was a fitting word for how all agents in the Stargate program had left the CIA. When Sheppard had been killed, he'd warned his agents with his dying breath, sending out a psychic message to cut and run, or they would suffer the same fate. They'd all gone to ground. "How much did Thomas tell you?"

"He told me nothing. Not a word."

"Then how…?" Had she bluffed in order to get him to spill the truth? Had she tricked him?

"I was cleaning out Thomas's old room and found something in a hiding place. He left it for me to find, I'm certain. You know that he's dead, don't you?"

"Yes, I'm sorry." But there was no time for grief. "What did he leave for you to find?"

"His CIA ID card. And there was a telephone number on a notepad. I called the number and spoke to this guy at the CIA. But he wouldn't tell me how Thomas died. All he said was that it was an accident during a training exercise. Do you know how he died? Were you with him?"

Jack shook his head. "I haven't seen Thomas since that day at the BBQ."

"But you were one of his closest friends, and you worked together. You were in the CIA together. How can—"

"The program we were in was top secret. We had to break up contact with everybody from our former lives. I never knew until two days ago that Thomas was recruited into the same program as I. And then we all had to go to ground three years ago. We're being hunted."

"Hunted? By whom?"

"By whoever killed our program leader, Henry Sheppard."

Surprise registered on Lilly's face. Then she shook her head. "You're lying."

The accusation stung. "I'm not lying. I'm telling you the truth."

"I spoke to Henry Sheppard. He's the person I called at the CIA. He told me he can't tell me how Thomas died because it was a matter of national security."

"I don't know who you spoke to, but it wasn't Henry Sheppard. Sheppard died over three years ago. He was murdered."

For a long moment he held her gaze. Her expression changed to one of realization. "That's why the page in the notebook was ripped out. And why the name was crossed out."

"What are you saying?" he asked.

"When I said I found a number and name on a little notepad, it's not quite... well, you know when you write something on a pad of paper and you're using a lot of pressure with your pen, it leaves an impression behind. I found a piece of paper with that kind of impression and used a pencil to reveal the name and number on it. I thought it was a clever way of Thomas leaving it for me without it being too obvious. As kids we did that all the time. But if Thomas knew that this Henry Sheppard was dead, then he probably just ripped out the page. After he crossed out the name and number."

"Makes sense. Can I see the notepad?"

She shook her head. "I left it at home. But I programmed the number into my phone." Then she cast him an annoyed glare. "And you tossed my phone out the car window."

"I had to do that, or whoever is after you would have been able to track us. Don't worry, if you called him from your cell phone, we can get the number via your phone carrier."

"Why would somebody try to kill me? Maybe the shooter at the plaza was just some random crazy. I mean, shootings like that happen all the time."

"Sure they do, but this wasn't a random shooting. You must have rattled somebody's cage when you called the fake Henry Sheppard and asked him about Thomas. What did you tell him?"

Lilly shrugged. "Just that I can't find a death certificate among my uncle's papers. Uncle Will has dementia, you know, so I cleaned out his house after he had to go into an assisted living facility."

Jack didn't interrupt her to let her know what he knew about Will Reed.

"I was in the Congo on a medical research trip when Thomas died, and I only just found out that he was cremated. And he never wanted to be cremated, because he was afraid—"

"—of fire, because of how his mother died," Jack completed her sentence.

"Exactly. And Uncle Will knew it. He would have never done this to Thomas. He would have respected his wishes. Turns out, Uncle Will never had a choice. According to the cremation certificate I found in Uncle Will's house, Thomas was cremated at a funeral home called Peaceful Rest. But when I went there to ask them about the cremation, they told me the cremation certificate was forged, and they had no record of Thomas being cremated there. And on top of it, when I called the funeral home where he was actually laid to rest, Shaded Pine Cemetery, they sent me a document that showed that Uncle Will bought the place in the urn wall and the maintenance plan. The document had his signature on it. Only, it was his signature from years ago, before he got that tremor in his hand. He couldn't have signed the document."

Jack was impressed with Lilly's research. "Did you tell this guy at the CIA about what you found?"

She nodded. "I asked for an explanation about the cremation certificate. But he doesn't know about Uncle Will's signature, because I got the call from Shaded Pine Cemetery just before I went down to the taco truck."

"That's why they want you gone. You were digging too deep. They don't want us to find out how and where Thomas died. Because it may lead us to them."

"Who are *they*?"

"Don't know. But I'll be damned if I don't give my all to find out."

"I already ordered Thomas's death certificate from the DC Vital Records Division but it's gonna take weeks before they'll send it. I don't know where else to look for it." She gave a hopeless shrug. "It's so frustrating. I've been spinning my wheels."

"I've got a way to get the death certificate quicker." He pulled his cell phone from his pocket.

She stared at it. "Oh, so you can have a cell phone but I can't?"

"It's a burner." He dialed the number he'd memorized for Fox.

"Yeah?" Fox answered almost immediately.

"It's Yankee."

"Hey, what's up?"

"I need you or Michelle to hack into the DC Vital Records Division and get me a death certificate for River."

"Ah shit, he's dead?"

"Not a hundred percent sure. That's why I need to look into it."

"Okay. Call you as soon as I have it."

10

———

"River?" Lilly asked the moment Jack disconnected the call. "Is that Thomas's code name?"

Jack nodded.

"And Yankee? That's you?"

"That's right."

"What was so special about the program you two were in that it had to be kept so secret that you couldn't even tell each other? And why would somebody hunt you because of it?" There were so many questions she had, but Jack seemed reluctant to answer, and she wasn't beyond playing dirty to get them. "I deserve answers. Damn it, Jack, if that night seven years ago meant anything at all to you, then please tell me what's going on. You can't just show up out of nowhere, save my life, and then keep your secrets to yourself."

She suddenly realized something. "How did you even know that there would be a shooting? At least tell me that."

Slowly, he nodded. Then he pointed to her legs. "Let me patch you up while we talk."

"Okay." She sat down on the couch, and Jack crouched down at her feet and started cleaning the abrasions on her knees with antiseptic. "Start already."

"I'm probably making a huge mistake by telling you all this, but frankly, I'm sick of hiding what I am."

His words struck her as odd, but she didn't interrupt him.

"I'm a precognitive, a person who has visions about future events, premonitions."

She froze. "No, that's not possible. Psychics don't exist. That's just a scam."

Jack moved his head from side to side. "Sometimes I wish it were, but today I'm glad that I am a precognitive, otherwise you'd be dead now."

All breath rushed from her lungs. "Are you saying you saw what would happen today?"

He nodded. "I had a vision of the sniper shooting you in the head. I saw you die. I tried to call you to warn you, but all I got on your phone was static."

"That was you? The call while I was waiting for the tacos?"

"Yes. I tried to tell you to run into the building, but you couldn't hear me. I think the same person who ordered the hit on you also scrambled your phone, maybe even bugged it. I'm not sure why, but perhaps he knew that I would try to warn you and—"

"How? How would he know that you'd try to save me?"

"I'm not the only precognitive. Everybody who was in the Stargate program at the CIA had the gift of foresight. Including Henry Sheppard. And there might be others. A few months ago, I met one of my fellow agents who'd gone bad, turned to the dark side, and I must assume there are others who also chose the wrong side. For all we know, whoever is trying to kill the former Stargate agents, might be a precognitive and therefore get glimpses of whatever we're planning."

"Oh my God, how can you fight against an enemy like that?"

"By banding together, by finding all former Stargate agents, men like Thomas, and fight as one. We're stronger together."

"That's why you're here. You were looking for Thomas."

"Yes. I spoke to your uncle to see if he knew anything."

"But he's got dementia. He can't help you. He's not right in his head anymore." It made her sad, but she couldn't ignore the truth.

"I saw that. But there were things he said that make me think that he knows something. He kept saying that it was his fault, that *she* tricked him. *She* lied to him. They sent *her*."

"*She*? Who is *she*?"

"I don't know yet. At first, I thought that Thomas may have faked his death. At least that's what I thought when I saw that he was cremated. But after speaking to your uncle and seeing his grief, I believe Thomas is truly dead. Still, I have to make sure, in case he's still out there, waiting for me to find him. And even if he's really dead, how and where he was killed, could help us find who's behind it all."

"If you can look into the future, don't you already know what will happen?"

"It doesn't work like that. We've never been able to figure out how to direct the visions. That was what the Stargate program was trying to do: train us to be able to direct our visions into the future at will. Have you ever heard of remote viewing?"

Lilly nodded. "Yeah, I read about it a few years ago. Wasn't that some secret spy program that didn't work?"

"That's right. The CIA ran the program in the early 90s, but the agents they recruited had no precognitive skills. Hence it failed. Henry Sheppard was already working for the CIA at the time, and he knew it would work, if only he could recruit agents who already had the gift of foresight. Just like he did. So he started the program up again, but not even the top bosses at the agency knew about it. I was part of that program."

"So you can see into the future, but you can't force it in a specific direction? Is that it?" She couldn't believe that she was even asking this. It sounded unreal, yet Jack looked serious, and judging by the fact that he'd clearly known about the shooting in advance and rescued her, he spoke the truth.

"I'm afraid so. I believe it's triggered by emotional responses. I had the vision about you dying when I was with your uncle and saw a photo that was taken at the BBQ seven years ago."

Jack put a Band-aid on Lilly's left knee. "There, that should do." Then he rose from his crouching position and took a seat next to her, though he left some space between them so their bodies didn't touch.

Lilly looked at him. His face had changed. He'd always been handsome, but this new face was different, even more intense than he'd been seven years ago. His eyes were still the same, still of a piercing blue, and his voice was just as irresistibly sexy as back then. How had she not immediately realized who he was? She should have recognized his body the moment he'd pushed her out of the line of fire and buried her beneath him. She'd felt safe, despite the initial shock, as if her body had recognized his, even though her mind hadn't.

"Why did you have plastic surgery? Did you have an accident?"

"No. When Sheppard was murdered and we all had to disappear, I figured it was my best option not to be recognized by my enemies. In hindsight, maybe it wasn't necessary, but what's done is done. Nobody has recognized me in the past three years since I've been on the run. I was able to stay in Washington D.C. because of my new face."

"You were here in D.C. the entire time?"

"Pretty much."

"Did we ever cross paths here?" she asked though she really wanted to ask whether he'd watched her from afar. Whether he'd longed for her like she'd longed for him.

"No." He smiled, but the expression was sad. "We never crossed paths. I might not have been able to stay hidden if I'd seen you."

His revelation surprised her. Did this mean that he'd been thinking back to their night together, longing for more? She shook off the thought. Jack wasn't a sentimental guy, at least Thomas had always said that about him.

"The temptation would have been too great." He took her hand and rubbed his thumb over the back of it.

She met his gaze and felt the same magnetic attraction that had drawn them together years earlier and culminated in a passionate night of lovemaking.

Jack's cell phone rang. He let go of her hand. "Yeah?"

Lilly sat close enough to hear the voice at the other end of the line.

"I got the death certificate. It says heart attack."

"Bullshit!" Lilly cursed.

"Who's that?"

Jack sighed and put the call on speaker. "That's River's cousin, Lilly. Lilly, meet Fox."

"Take me off speaker now," Fox demanded. "You can't just let a civilian—"

"She's as much a civilian as Phoebe and Michelle are," Jack interrupted, though Lilly had no idea what he meant by that.

"Why didn't you say so? Hey, Lilly. And you're right, it's bullshit. Thomas was thirty-seven years old. There's no way he died of a heart attack," Fox said.

"Can you text me the document?" Jack asked. "Maybe I can talk to the doctor or medical examiner who signed the death certificate."

"Sending it over now. Do you need backup?"

"To talk to the official who signed the death certificate? No. I've got it handled. Be in touch."

"Check in every few hours so we know you're still alive."

"Will do." Jack disconnected the call.

A moment later, his cell phone chimed, announcing a text message. Jack opened the attachment.

"What does it say?" Lilly asked.

"He died here in D.C." Jack looked at her. "I'm gonna go and have a talk with this Dr. Amy Price who signed the death certificate. Stay here. Feel free to raid the fridge and the freezer while I'm gone."

"No way!" She jumped up. "You can't just bench me. Thomas was my cousin and my best friend. I'm coming with you."

"Not a chance. Whoever hired the sniper will be looking for you. You can't show your face outside. It's too risky."

"Then lend me a hat and sunglasses, or something."

He hesitated for several long seconds. Then he sighed. "Fine, but you'll do exactly as I say. Do we understand each other?"

"I'm not an idiot."

Less than half an hour later, Lilly's blond hair was hidden under a dark wig that made her look like Cher and itched like hell. But that was only part of the disguise Jack had insisted on as a condition of her accompanying him. Glasses that were too old-fashioned for her own grandmother to wear sat on her nose. She wore a poofy blouse and an ugly skirt that made her look twenty pounds overweight.

"I look ridiculous," she complained.

"No, you don't. You look like a wallflower. Nobody is gonna give you a second look, which is the point."

Jack had changed his clothing too, and now looked like an accountant. He sported a pair of glasses with metal frames and had donned a wig of thinning hair that showed an overly high widow's peak and a bald spot on top.

"How do I look?" he suddenly asked with a Midwestern accent.

"As ridiculous as I feel."

"Well, then, your chariot awaits."

He winked at her, and they got in the van. This time, Lilly sat in the front cabin with him. While Lilly had gotten changed, Jack had found the address where Dr. Amy Price worked.

"It's almost evening," Lilly said as they drove through a busy neighborhood. "What if that doctor isn't at the morgue anymore?"

"I also found her home address." He gave her a reassuring look.

After fifteen minutes, Jack turned into a parking garage that looked familiar.

"Isn't that where you changed cars earlier?" she asked.

"Yes. We'll leave the van here and take a different car."

"Don't you think that's a little paranoid?"

"Paranoid kept me alive for the last three years."

When they exited the van, Jack ushered her down the stairs a level farther below. There, he walked along the parked cars, looking at each of them.

"You don't remember where you parked your car?" she asked.

He gave her a sideways glance. "Oh, I don't have a car here." Then he pointed to a rather dusty looking silver Honda. "That one will do. It looks like it's been here forever. Nobody's gonna miss it."

She stared at him, shocked. "You're gonna steal that car?"

"Of course not."

Before she could sigh with relief, he added, "I'm just gonna borrow it."

She watched, in equal parts shocked and impressed, as he skillfully broke into the car and then hotwired the engine. Moments later, they were leaving the garage in the *borrowed* Honda, and headed for the morgue.

They were hitting rush hour traffic as they got closer. There was nothing they could do to go any faster. Lilly looked at the clock on the dashboard.

"We're almost there," Jack said.

Suddenly police sirens blared, and the cars behind them were making space, driving as close to the sidewalks as possible, so the police car could pass. Lilly's heart beat into her throat.

"They found us because you stole a car," Lilly said, panicked.

"Stay calm," Jack said and looked into the rear-view mirror. "They're not after us. There's an ambulance following the police car. There must have been an accident."

When both the police car and the ambulance passed them without stopping, Lilly's heartbeat returned to normal. Shit, she wasn't made for a life of crime.

A block before the morgue, a police car was blocking the street. Jack saw it and turned into the closest side street.

"We'll have to walk from here," he said and parked in the nearest parking spot he could find.

"Are you not worried about having to walk past the police?" Lilly asked.

"The police are the least of my worries. Just act normal."

They exited the car and walked back to where the police were blocking the street that led to the Medical Examiner's building. Lots of curious pedestrians were already flocking to the scene.

"Can you see what's going on?" Lilly asked Jack, who was much taller than her.

"Looks like a pedestrian got hit by a car." He reached for her hand. "Let's get through here."

Jack made his way through the crowd, Lilly following him closely. Lilly glanced to the street where the ambulance was parked and police officers cordoned off the scene.

They were only about fifty feet away from the entrance to the Medical Examiner's building now. From there, people exited and ran out toward the ambulance.

Lilly could hear a woman cry out. "Oh, no! Amy!"

Jack suddenly stopped and looked over his shoulder at the person lying on the ground in the middle of the street. He pushed through the bystanders, still holding on to Lilly's hand, until he reached the cordon. From there, Lilly could see that the person on the ground was a woman.

"What happened?" Jack asked somebody next to him.

"Hit 'n' run," the man next to him said.

"Do you know who it is?"

"No idea. But I think she came out of the building behind us."

Lilly froze. The building behind them was the Medical Examiner's office.

"Let me through!" a woman called out from behind them, and pushed through the crowd, until she reached the cordon next to Lilly. "Oh my God! Amy!"

"Do you know her?" Lilly asked the tearful woman.

The woman sobbed. "It's my colleague, Dr. Price. I saw it from my office window." She let out a heart-rending sob. "The car didn't even try to stop..."

Lilly looked back at the scene on the street, where a police officer put a sheet over the victim. Dr. Amy Price was dead.

11

———

Jack knew immediately that Dr. Amy Price's death was no accident or coincidence. Somebody had killed her so she wouldn't reveal how Thomas Reed had really died. Whether Dr. Price had been complicit in Thomas's death, or coerced into signing a death certificate with a fake cause of death, was immaterial. The result was the same: now only the killer knew how Thomas had died.

Jack drove Lilly back to the safe house, using the same precautions as before and wiping his and Lilly's fingerprints from the borrowed car. Then Jack contacted Ace and Fox to update them on what had happened, and to ask them to review any traffic cameras in the vicinity of the Medical Examiner's building to see if they would provide any leads on Dr. Price's killer.

Then Jack drove back to the plaza where Lilly had nearly been killed. It was dark now, and quiet, though the police had cordoned off the area of the shooting. Jack didn't approach but remained on the opposite side of the street, not wanting to be noticed. For what he needed to do, he didn't need to be too close. He looked around and surveilled the area. There were no traffic cameras, although there were several security cameras at the entrances and exits of the Delta

Labs building where Lilly worked. However, they were pointing too low, and if Jack's assumptions were correct, the shooter had been aiming at Lilly from a higher perch.

Judging by the direction of the bullet, the shooter had been in an above-ground parking garage. Jack went to the garage and checked all five levels for any signs such as spent casings from the sniper's rifle, but while he found imprints of a tripod on a ledge that had a clear view of the plaza, he found nothing else. The sniper had cleaned up. This was a bust.

It was past ten o'clock when he returned to the safe house. In the garage, he rid himself of his disguise then entered the house. Jack closed the door quietly. Only the lights from the kitchen illuminated the living room dimly. Lilly lay on the couch, now dressed in her own clothes again, sleeping. The wig and glasses lay on the coffee table, and the clothes that had turned her into a shapeless woman, were neatly folded on a chair.

He treaded lightly and approached Lilly. There was a peaceful expression on her face, and it reminded him of the day when he'd snuck out of the hotel room, while she was still sleeping.

He reached for a blanket, and spread it over her, when she suddenly shrieked and sat up. Jack stepped back and raised his hands. "Sorry, I didn't mean to wake you."

Her eyes focused on him. "No, no, it's fine, I just... I'm just a little on edge." She took a deep breath. "I can't believe somebody killed that woman just so she couldn't tell us how Thomas died."

"I know. But the people after me and after all Stargate agents are unscrupulous."

She reached for his hand and motioned him to sit next to her. "I can't imagine how you and Thomas must have lived for the last three years. It's not even been a day for me, and already I'm a nervous wreck."

"Thomas and I were trained for this. You're a civilian."

"Still, no matter the training, I can't imagine how the last three years must have been for you."

He noticed the look she gave him. It was one of understanding. He held her gaze. "It's been a lonely time, I admit." When she seemed to move her head closer to his, he added, "And every day since that night, I regretted that I had to leave you. I missed you..."

"You broke my heart, Jack," she murmured softly. "For a long time, I was so angry with you for leaving without a word..." She rubbed her fingertips over his cheek.

He took her hand and turned it so he could press a kiss into her palm. "I'm sorry that I hurt you. I wish it could have been different... but the visions I had, the things I saw, I needed to understand them, and Henry Sheppard gave me that. I was able to save lives, to prevent catastrophes because of what I saw. Had I not accepted Sheppard's offer—"

She put her finger over his lips. "You don't have to justify your decision. I understand now. I understand why you had to leave. I wish I'd known back then. It would still have broken my heart to let you go, but I wouldn't have been angry with you."

"Thank you," he said, his heart warming with the knowledge that she was full of forgiveness. "Not a day went by where I didn't think of you." He pulled back, because the temptation to kiss her was growing too strong. "And as much as I wanted to be with you, I couldn't ask you to live like this... on the run... always hiding. You have a life. A career. I couldn't drag you into this."

Lilly shook her head. "That was then. But now it's different. I'm already in the middle of it. At least with you, I feel safe. I would be dead without you."

She nudged closer, and Jack became more and more aware of the effect she had on him. Her nearness was fanning his desire for her, his need to have her beneath him, to feel her skin against his, her lips on his, his cock inside her.

"Lilly..." He dipped his head to hers. "You have to stop me, before it's too late, because I can't promise you anything. I can't offer you the life you deserve."

"I don't care about that. I only care about you. About how you made me feel seven years ago. We had something. And I want it back. Please don't deny me that. Jack..."

Lilly brushed her index finger over his lower lip. Her touch felt electrifying. His brain suddenly stopped working, and all he could think of was what her lips would taste like.

"I could never deny you anything," he whispered against her lips before he captured them and kissed her.

She tasted sweet, and only now he took in her scent fully and realized that she'd taken a shower in his absence. Her mouth was warm and supple, but so very different from how she'd kissed him back seven years ago. The woman he held in his arms tonight was more demanding, not the almost timid girl he'd taken to his bed such a long time ago, but an experienced woman who knew what she wanted. He felt it with every fiber of his being, felt the passion and desire she now unleashed as if she'd stored it up for him all these years.

His own desire matched hers, because he too had felt something special back then. In truth, he'd been in love with her even before he'd ever met her. Thomas had talked so much about her during their deployments that he'd felt he knew her. He knew about her likes and dislikes, her compassion, and her dreams. Her dream of becoming a doctor and helping people, was one of the reasons he'd never tried to reconnect with her after he'd entered the CIA. She would have had to give it all up. For him. And he hadn't wanted her to make that sacrifice. But circumstances had thrust them back together, and neither of them had a choice now. But he didn't want to think of the difficulties that lay ahead.

He wanted to feel Lilly. With her in his arms, with her body pressed to his, he felt that the flame they'd ignited seven years earlier had never extinguished. It had burned beneath the surface for all those years. It flared up now and grew into a massive bonfire, one that could only be extinguished one way: by stoking it even higher.

Jack ripped his lips from hers. "Lilly..." He didn't know what he wanted to say, because all he could think of was undressing her so he could feel her naked skin under his lips and hands.

"Take your clothes off," Lilly demanded, her eyes locking with his.

"You first." Jack started undressing her.

But she couldn't be deterred. She opened the buttons of his dress shirt and ripped it open. When she put her hands on his chest, his heart seemed to go up in flames. He'd dreamed of her touch so many times in the past years without hope of ever having another chance at being with Lilly. He'd resigned himself to that fate. But now, he couldn't accept it any longer. He needed her back in his life.

Jack pulled Lilly's top over her head and tossed it on the coffee table. When his gaze fell onto the black lace bra she wore, his breath hitched. Her creamy flesh invited him to explore her. He dipped his head to her breasts, not giving her a chance to continue undressing him. He pressed kisses to the valley between her breasts, then cupped them with his hands, before sliding his thumbs underneath the fabric and caressing her nipples. They were hard little buds, responding to his touch.

Lilly gasped. "Jack..."

Impatiently, he pushed the straps aside so he could slide his hands fully beneath the cups of her bra, taking possession of her beautiful breasts. He kneaded them in his hands, loving the feel of making her moan with pleasure.

Lilly dropped her head back, surrendering to his touch, and he kissed her soft skin. The bra suddenly fell away, and Jack realized that Lilly had opened the clasp behind her back.

He pressed Lilly back so she came to lie on the sofa, then reached for her skirt, opened the zipper and pulled it off her. She wore only a pair of tiny panties. Lilly looked at him, beckoning him to take her. It took a few more moments, before he'd finally rid himself of his own clothes. His boxer briefs and her panties were the only barriers left now. He looked at her and drank in the sight, before he freed her of her panties.

Like an offering, she lay in front of him, completely naked, her nipples hard, her skin glistening. He could sense her arousal and dipped his head between her legs to taste her. She gasped, surprised, and her pelvis tilted toward him, welcoming his mouth and tongue exploring her. She tasted like a fresh spring morning after the rain, and he let himself fall into the fantasy that they would one day have a life together.

Behind his boxer briefs, his cock pressed against its prison, demanding to be freed, but he couldn't allow it, despite his own growing need.

Beneath him, Lilly moaned and called out his name. He teased her with his tongue, swiped it against her center of pleasure and felt her arousal climbing higher. She rubbed herself against his mouth.

"Jack! Please, I need you inside me."

He lifted his head for a moment. "Lilly, I can't. I don't have any condoms here."

She lifted her head and stared at him. "Goddamn it, Jack." Then she suddenly laughed. "I'm on the pill."

He smirked. "Why didn't you say that earlier?"

"You didn't ask."

He lifted himself off her and took off his boxer briefs. His fully erect cock jutted out.

"Hmm," she said and licked her lips.

Before he could stop her, she sat up and put her lips around the tip of his cock, taking him deep into her warm mouth.

"Fuck, Lilly!"

For a few seconds he let her suck him and enjoyed her masterful touch. But then he pulled himself out of her mouth. "You're playing with a loaded weapon, baby."

"Then maybe you should use it on me." She cast him a coquettish look.

"As you wish."

He pressed her back onto the couch and settled between her thighs, before he nudged his cock at her pussy. He felt her wetness and warmth, while she slid her hands onto his hips and pulled him to her. He thrust into her, seating himself to the hilt. Closing his eyes, he let out a breath.

"Fuck!"

When he opened his eyes, he looked straight into Lilly's. She smiled at him.

"I missed you," she murmured.

"I missed you more."

With long thrusts, he started to ride her, while he sank his lips onto hers. Their bodies moved in synch as if they'd done this a million times, when in truth they'd only had one night together. But just like seven years ago, they clicked. He'd never before experienced anything like it with a woman. He'd never felt the connection that he felt with Lilly with anybody else. She seemed to know instinctively what he wanted and needed, just like he knew how to pleasure her without her needing to tell him. Everything felt perfect, as if they were made for each other.

Lilly's interior muscles gripped him like a tight fist, and her wetness felt like sliding into warm silk. He couldn't get enough of it, and bit back the urge to climax. No, he needed to make the most of it, to prolong the pleasure they were giving each other, because he didn't know whether they would have another day, or week, or month. He needed to live a whole life in this one night, and it felt like Lilly knew it too. Either one of them could die tomorrow or the next day. Life wasn't certain, but their connection was.

He wasn't a man of many words, didn't know how to tell Lilly what he felt for her, but he could show her with his body.

When he couldn't hold onto his control any longer, he looked into her eyes. "Lilly," he murmured, not finding the words she deserved. That he loved her; that he had always loved her. But those words carried a promise, one he couldn't make for fear he would be forced to break it one day.

Lilly shuddered underneath him, and Jack let himself go and spilled his seed in her, thrusting hard and deep. As they both stilled and their breathing settled into a slower rhythm, Jack brushed a featherlight kiss on her lips and caressed her face.

"Jack?"

"Yes?"

"I know you can't make me any promises... but..."

"But what?" he asked softly hoping whatever she wanted from him was within his power to grant.

"Promise me that you'll be here tomorrow morning. Just this once I want to wake up with you."

"I'll be here. But I can't promise you that we'll wake up together." He winked. "That would imply that we're actually going to get any sleep. And that I can't guarantee." He slowly moved his still semi-hard cock back and forth. "Unless you've had enough."

Lilly put both hands on his ass to hold him close to her. "I'm ready for round two, but if you need a break, I'll wait."

He chuckled. "Give me five minutes, and I'm all yours."

12

———

Lilly was awake with a start. For a moment, she had no idea where she was. It was still dark, though a little bit of light seemed to enter the room from the sides of the blinds. The bed wasn't hers, but the warmth in it felt familiar and safe. Then she remembered the past twelve hours.

Next to her, Jack's naked body glistened with sweat, and he fidgeted in his sleep. Moans came from him, and she realized that he was in the throes of a nightmare.

PTSD? Very likely. After all, he'd been a soldier deployed in war zones around the world before he'd joined the CIA.

Lilly switched on the bedside lamp, casting a warm light on the bed. She put her hands on Jack's shoulders to wake him gently. But he continued mumbling something unintelligible and moved his head from side to side. Beneath her palms, his muscles tightened, and all of a sudden, he shook off her hands, grabbed her and tossed her on her back. All air rushed from Lilly's lungs.

"Jack, stop!" she cried out.

He suddenly froze, still hovering above her. It took another second before his eyes focused, and he appeared to recognize her.

With a curse, he let go of her and sat back on his heels.

"Fuck! Lilly, I'm so sorry. Did I hurt you?"

She sat up, still a little shaken, but no worse for wear. "No, you didn't. I'm fine. You had a nightmare."

He took a few quick breaths. "Not a nightmare. A premonition."

"Oh! You have them in your sleep?" she asked, curious, since he hadn't talked much about this subject earlier.

"No."

"But—"

"What I mean to say is not normally. My premonitions come to me when I'm awake. This is the only one that comes in my sleep. And it's not the first time."

"Are you saying you get the same vision repeatedly?"

"This one yes. And I'm not the only one who gets them. The other Stargate agents get them too. But nobody has yet figured out what they mean."

"What do you all see?"

"That's just it, we all see something different, but we know we're seeing the same thing."

She wrinkled her forehead. "Uhm, that doesn't make sense. How would you know that if you all see something different?"

"It's a sense we all get. We know it's the end game, a big event that we're meant to prevent."

It sounded ominous. "What kind of event?"

"We're not sure. There is a massive explosion, dead bodies, a shockwave..." He ran a shaking hand through his hair. "I feel an explosion..." He hesitated. "Somewhere in Washington D.C. I see the White House, and then I feel a shockwave, indicating that the explosion is happening somewhere behind me, but the moment I turn around, the premonition ends."

Now she was trembling and instinctively pulled the duvet closer to her naked body. "Do all your premonitions come true?"

He nodded. "So far, yes. That is, unless I interfere and change the outcome like I did yesterday. I haven't always been able to stop what happened in my premonitions, particularly not during the last three years. There's a risk."

She stared at him. "What kind of risk?"

"That I'll be recognized."

"But you had plastic surgery. Not even I recognized you."

"Not recognized by my face, but by what I do: prevent an impending disaster. Whoever is hunting Stargate agents is watching the news for people who might have had prior knowledge of an accident or some other calamity and intervenes."

Her heart beat frantically now. "Do you think somebody saw that you saved me from the shooter yesterday?"

For a moment, Jack was silent, contemplating his answer. "Yes, the shooter did. That's why I had to get you out of there quickly and change cars. I'm sure he's already reported to his boss what I did. And Mr. Smith has most likely already put two and two together and realized that I'm one of the men he's hunting."

"Wait! Mr. Smith? You know who he is?"

"No. But we know that he calls himself Smith, because Fox's girlfriend had contact with him."

"So she knows what he looks like."

"I'm afraid not. He made sure she never laid eyes on him."

"Shit." Then she remembered something else. "But that means Smith now knows what your new face looks like. I mean if the shooter saw it."

"There's a chance, yes, but since there were no cameras, I doubt he got a very good look even if he saw me through his scope. He was too busy aiming at you." He swung his legs out of bed. "But we need to take extra precautions from now on."

"What are you planning?"

"We need to see Ace and Fox. Let's shower and get ready."

She nodded. "I guess that means I won't be able to go back to my apartment to pick up some of my stuff."

He tossed her a regretful look. "I'm afraid not. I'll try and get you what you need some other way."

"Alright," she said, swallowing hard, but accepting the fact that her normal life was over, and her career would go down the drain, wasn't easy.

Maybe when all this was over, when Jack and his friends had found the mysterious Mr. Smith and stopped him, life would go back to normal. With one difference: she and Jack would have a chance at a life together.

For now, all she had were the few items she carried in her purse. It wasn't much, but it would have to do for now.

They showered and dressed. While Jack went into the garage, Lilly made coffee. She poured herself a cup, then poured one for Jack. He was still in the garage, so she opened the door and joined him.

She found him at the back of the van, crouching down and screwing a license plate onto the van. "What are you doing?" she asked when she handed him the coffee mug.

"Changing out the license plate just in case it was somehow spotted."

"But you've been so careful. You didn't use the van to come to Delta Labs. You used a different car." One that was most likely also *borrowed* like the one they'd used to get to the Medical Examiner's building.

"If whoever is after you is checking the traffic cams, they might have tracked us to the parking garage where we changed cars. It's possible that they followed all other cars exiting the garage when they realized that I dumped the Toyota there. Though I've tried to use routes that don't have a lot of cameras."

"So you think they might have the license plate number?"

Jack took a sip from his coffee. "Yeah. And they'll be on the lookout for a white van." He walked around the van, then opened a large storage cupboard.

Lilly looked at the interior. "What are those?"

"Decals," Jack said and rummaged through the items. "I need to disguise the van. Can't leave it plain white. The more I can make it look different the better." He pulled several large decals out of the cupboard. "Wanna give me a hand?"

"Sure." She placed her coffee mug on the workbench.

Jack handed her a decal the size of a large briefcase. It had a phone number printed on it, as well as the symbol of a Staff of Asclepius, a universal medical sign.

"You're making it look like an ambulance?" she asked doubtfully.

"Not an ambulance." He stuck a much larger sign on one of the sides of the van and pointed to it. "Medical transport. It'll be perfect for where we're going."

"Which is?"

"A rehab facility."

"For alcoholics?"

"You'll see."

13

———————

This time, Jack didn't exchange the van for a car in a parking garage. Instead, they drove for about half an hour, making lots of detours, which Jack said were necessary to make sure they weren't being tailed, until they finally stopped in front of an iron gate.

Lilly read the sign.

Sober Living Rehabilitation Center.

Behind the gates, she spotted a large old villa surrounded by a lush looking garden with mature trees and bushes. Lilly looked at Jack, who pulled out his cell phone. They hadn't talked much on the drive. Jack had been concentrating on traffic and constantly looked into the rear-view mirror, trying to spot if they had a tail, as he called it.

"Hey, Ace," Jack said into the phone. "Mind opening the gate? We're right outside."

There was a short pause, then Jack said, "Yes, Lilly is with me."

He disconnected the call, and an instant later, the iron gate slid to the side, opening for them. Jack put the van in gear and drove through it. Instead of stopping in front of the house, he drove around the left side past a couple of large trees, until a free-standing garage came into view. Jack stopped the van in front of it and killed the engine.

He looked at her and squeezed her hand. "Come, let me introduce you to everybody."

They exited the car and approached the house from the back. A door opened and revealed a handsome dark-haired man waiting for them. He looked like he was in his mid to late thirties. His attire was casual, yet his gaze was vigilant.

Instead of a greeting, he addressed Jack. "You made sure nobody followed you?"

"Took a few detours. We're in the clear."

"Nice touch with the van," he said and pointed to it. Then he gave Lilly a long look, before he extended his hand in greeting. "I'm Ace. But you can call me Scott. Nice to meet you, Lilly. Sorry about your loss."

Lilly shook his hand. "Thank you."

"Let's get inside," Ace suggested, and quickly they entered and closed the door behind them.

They were in a large eat-in kitchen that looked like it could seat an army. It was clean, except for a few coffee mugs on the counter. The smell of bacon hung in the air, making Lilly hungry all of a sudden. The previous night, she'd snacked on a few crackers and cheese while she'd waited for Jack to return. And the cup of coffee this morning hadn't exactly filled her belly either.

"Hungry?" Jack asked.

"It's okay," she said quickly.

As Ace led them through the kitchen, they entered a large foyer. Lilly glanced around. It was quiet, as if the house was deserted.

"This is not a rehab facility, is it?" she asked.

"Only on the outside," Ace said. "It keeps curious neighbors away." Then he pointed to a door. "This way."

But when they reached the door, a female voice came from the stairs.

"Hey Jack, you brought Lilly, huh?"

Lilly pivoted to see a pregnant young woman walking down the stairs.

"Didn't really have a choice," Jack said. "The assassin will try again."

"Lilly," Ace said, "meet my fiancée, Phoebe."

Lilly noticed Phoebe's soft smile when she looked at Ace. Then she ripped her gaze from him and approached Lilly.

"So nice to meet you."

"Nice to meet you too, Phoebe."

"May I ask you for a favor?" Jack asked, addressing Phoebe. "Lilly can't go back to her place, and she has nothing else on her apart from her handbag—"

"Say no more," Phoebe interrupted. "Between Michelle and me, we'll have plenty of clothes and shoes to lend her." Then she smiled at Lilly. "You're about my size." She chuckled. "Or what my size used to be before this." She put a hand on her pregnant belly.

"Thank you, that's so kind of you."

"Why don't you take Lilly upstairs," Ace suggested, "while we get caught up on things?"

"Come with me," Phoebe said.

Lilly hesitated.

"It's all right," Jack said. "You're safe here." He glanced at Ace. "Does your offer to crash here still stand?"

"Absolutely." Ace looked at his fiancée. "Can you please get them settled in the front guest room?"

"Sure. Come," Phoebe said.

This time, Lilly followed her invitation, and side by side, they walked up the large staircase.

"This is a gorgeous house," Lilly remarked.

"Yes, isn't it? It belongs to Scott."

"Is it only the two of you who live here? I mean, it's not a rehab center, right? That's just a front," Lilly added.

"Yes, it's just the two of us... and soon this little boy will join us."

"You already know the sex of the baby? I didn't realize they could tell this early on. You can't be more than five months along."

"You've got a good eye," Phoebe said. "I know the sex of the baby only because Scott had a premonition. He already knows what our little boy will look like."

As Phoebe opened the door to a large bedroom, Lilly said, "I'm still trying to get used to the fact that true psychics exist."

"Well, they like to be called precognitives, but yes, they are psychic. Just as well, or I wouldn't even be here."

Lilly looked at Phoebe. "What happened?"

Phoebe walked to a large walk-in closet, and Lilly followed her.

"Some psycho locked me and two dozen kids in a school bus and stopped it on the train tracks."

"Oh my God!"

"Scott had a premonition about it, and he saved me and every single child. I still shudder at what could have happened, if he hadn't made it in time."

"I can only imagine how terrified you and your students must have been. So you're a teacher?"

She laughed and shook her head. "I wouldn't have the patience for a class full of third graders. No, I'm a reporter. Well, I was, before I had to go into hiding with Scott."

Lilly nodded. "Yeah, guess I'm in hiding now too."

"Scott told me what happened yesterday after Jack called him. And then I saw the news report later. You must be shaken."

"At first it was all adrenaline, and I didn't really know what was happening. It all sank in later, you know?"

"It always does. But you're here now, and we'll keep you safe." Then she pointed to the clothes. "Now let's see if some of these things fit you. You're in luck too: I just ordered new underwear and it's still in its original packaging. You can take those. And I'm sure Michelle has a few things too that might work for you. What's your shoe size?"

"I'm a 7 ½."

"I'm an eight, but I think Michelle might be your size."

"Did I hear my name?" the voice of a woman came from the bedroom.

"We're in the walk-in closet, Michelle," Phoebe called out.

A moment later, a thirty-something woman with dark hair popped her head in. "Hey! You must be Lilly. I'm Michelle, Nick's girlfriend."

"Hi, Michelle, nice to meet you." Lilly shook her hand.

"The guys said you were up here going through clothes," Michelle said.

"Yeah," Phoebe said, "Lilly can't go home, so she needs a few things. She wears size 7 ½ shoes. What's your size?"

"Sorry, I'm a six. Let's order you a few pairs of shoes," Michelle suggested, and already pulled out her cell phone and started typing on it. "Let's get you some tennis shoes, some sandals..."

She looked at Lilly's shoes which were pumps she wore to work, but which by now made her feet hurt.

"Yeah, you probably don't want anything too dressy. I always vote for sensible shoes, just in case you've gotta run." Michelle and Phoebe exchanged a look.

"I agree," Phoebe said.

"Okay," Lilly said. "Let me give you my credit card for the order."

She dug into her handbag, but Michelle put her hand on her arm to stop her.

"You might as well forget that you have a credit card. You can't use it anymore, or somebody will track you down."

"But then how, I mean, what am I gonna do for money?"

"I'll take care of it," Michelle said.

"But I can't just take your money."

Michelle smirked. "Oh, it's not my money."

Lilly stared at her, confused. "Then whose money is it?"

"Some Russian oligarchs' or that of some other rich people

who've lost track of how much they have," Michelle said lightly. "I rotate things around so nobody gets wind of what I'm doing."

"How?"

"I'm a hacker. It's really pretty simple when you know what to do." She shrugged.

"And it's a godsend," Phoebe said. "Otherwise, Scott and I wouldn't be able to maintain this house for very long. We were pretty broke until about a week ago, when we found Nick and Michelle. The house belongs to Scott, though it's not in his name so that his enemies can't find him, but it's not like either one of us can hold down a job, not while Scott's on the run. And we had to spend quite a bit on beefing up security here. The place was deserted for years after his father was murdered."

"His father? Was he in the CIA too?"

"Yes, he ran the program Scott, Nick, and Jack were in."

"Are you saying Henry Sheppard was Scott's father?"

Phoebe nodded. "His adoptive father."

No wonder Jack had been so certain that the man Lilly had spoken to on the phone hadn't been Henry Sheppard.

Lilly let out a breath. "This is all so overwhelming."

Phoebe gave her a kind smile. "How about we make some tea and have a snack, and we'll fill you in on everything you need to know?"

"That sounds perfect," Lilly replied.

14

_____

In the nerve center of the mansion, the computer room with the dark gray paint, Jack filled in Ace and Fox about everything he'd discovered in his search for Thomas Reed, starting with his visit to River's father in the nursing home and the old man's odd ramblings, his premonition about Lilly's would-be assassination, and ending with the hit-and-run death of Dr. Amy Price.

"Fuck!" Ace cursed. "That doctor definitely knew something our enemies don't want us to find. There must be a report or something that she wrote down before she issued the death certificate. There should be something in her files."

Fox was already sitting at his computer, tapping away on his keyboard. He was a talented hacker, and even though Jack had a few skills like that too, Fox was a pro. "I'm checking. Give me a minute or two to get into their system."

Meanwhile, Jack and Ace continued talking.

"So you think Thomas is really dead?" Ace asked.

Jack nodded. "I'm afraid so. If he'd been only faking his death, then Dr. Price would still be alive. No, it's pretty clear to me now that he was killed by Smith and his cronies. And they don't want us to find out what the manner of his death was. Otherwise, there would be no reason to kill the pathologist who signed the death certificate, nor fake the cremation certificate. Or to cremate him in the first place, when I know he was against cremation. They didn't want us to find the body, because it would help us figure out what happened."

"And probably lead us to Smith. I agree," Ace said. "The question is how." He looked over his shoulder to where Fox was working. "Anything?"

"Looking through the file folders now," Fox said. "But at first glance, there's nothing on Thomas Reed. I've searched all folders. If there was a file about an autopsy performed there under Dr. Price's supervision, then somebody's deleted it. Though my guess? There was no file in the first place."

Jack nodded. "Makes sense. They don't want a paper trail about River's manner of death. And with Dr. Price dead, this is a dead end."

"Fox, can you think of anything else that would help us figure out where River was or what he did in the weeks before his death?" Ace asked.

Fox turned away from the computer. "If he had a cell phone on him, even if it was a burner, as long as we know the number, we'd have a chance of tracking his whereabouts. But you guys know as well as I do, that he would have been more careful and not have exposed his number to anybody he didn't trust."

"That's it," Jack said. "Maybe he called Lilly. They were close." He rose. "Let me get her." Before he reached the door, there was a soft pinging sound coming from a speaker on the ceiling.

"Michelle, can you please bring Lilly down to the computer room?" Fox said through the intercom.

Jack cast him a look. "Neat."

Ace smiled. "Saves us a lot of running around."

"You must have made a lot of upgrades to the house. Can't have been cheap," Jack commented.

"I put all my money into it, but maintaining this house is

another matter." Ace pointed to Fox. "Luckily this guy and his girlfriend had a brilliant idea: steal from the rich to support a good cause."

"The good cause being getting Stargate back together," Fox interjected.

"Are you saying you're hacking rich people's bank accounts to finance all this?" Jack asked.

Fox grinned. "Not just any rich people; rich people who hide their money from the tax man. So, we're really government funded, because the money we siphon off would have gone to the IRS."

"You're a veritable Robin Hood." Jack laughed. "Ace, what did you do for money until Fox and Michelle came along? I mean, they only showed up on your radar ten days ago."

"Believe it or not, I repaired motorcycles for over three years and saved every penny. And there was a little money left from my father. It paid for all the legal maneuvering I had to do to keep this house and make sure nobody knows I still own it." Then he tipped his chin toward Jack. "How about you? How did you keep your head above water?"

"Well, after spending my last dime on plastic surgery so I could stay in D.C., I freelanced for a bail bondsman whenever I needed cash."

"Bounty hunter?" Fox asked and shook his head. "Why didn't I think of that? Instead, I was slaving away as a freelance website designer."

"You probably made better money doing that than the occasional bounties I brought in," Jack said.

The door suddenly opened, and Lilly entered. "Hey."

"Lilly, this is Fox," Jack said.

"You can call me Nick," he said and raised his hand in greeting.

"Hey, Nick. Nice to meet you." Then she looked at Jack. "You wanted to see me?"

"Yes, we were just talking about Thomas and wondering if he called you in the weeks before his death," Jack said.

"The last call I got from him was about two weeks before his death, I think."

"Did you see the number that he called you from?" Jack asked.

"No, his calls always showed up as Private Caller or Unknown Number."

"You sure?"

Lilly sighed. "I'm sure, and I would show you my call history, but you tossed my cell phone out of the car."

Jack started on an apology. "Uhm—"

But Fox interrupted him. "No worries, I can check on that if you give me your number. In the meantime, Jack said that you found your cousin's ID and Henry Sheppard's number in a hiding place meant for you?"

"That's right."

"Was that all he left you? No other documents? Nothing else?" Fox asked.

"No that's all...uhm, except for an empty memory stick. Sorry that I can't be of more help—"

"An empty memory stick?" Fox asked, sounding excited. "Do you still have it?"

"But it's empty. I checked it myself."

"It might not be empty," Fox said. "Did you keep it?"

"I think I put it in my handbag." She opened her bag and rummaged through it. After an eternity, she produced a USB flash drive. "This is it."

She handed it to Fox who immediately put it into a USB port and started typing away on his keyboard. Jack approached and looked over his shoulder to the screen.

"You're looking for a hidden file folder?" Jack asked.

"Yep. River got the same training as the rest of us. While he might not have been a computer genius like myself"—Ace chuckled from behind them—"he would have known the basics about how to hide a directory so it looks like the flash drive is empty."

All of a sudden, a window opened up on the screen, and a beep sounded.

"Voilà!" Fox said. "Just like I thought. All we need now is a password."

Lilly came to stand next to Jack to look at the screen. "Wow. You were right."

"Yep, it happens a lot," Fox said.

"Can you click on that, where it says password hint?" she asked.

Fox clicked on it, and a question popped up. "What rabbit but an old one has his foot in a pot without a lid?" he read aloud. "That makes no fucking sense."

"Oh my God, our code," Lilly said, shock registering on her face.

"What code?" Jack asked.

"When we were kids, Thomas and I developed this code to send each other secret messages, basically emails that needed a password. And the hint was always in the subject line." She shook her head, tears suddenly brimming in her eyes. "Thomas was right. He knew it all along."

"Knew what?" Jack asked.

"At the time, I thought it was silly. He said that one day I would need a password, and he wouldn't be there to give it to me. I would have to figure it out on my own. He was the one who came up with the game. He drilled it into me." She locked eyes with Jack. "He saw it. He saw it back then. It all makes sense now."

Jack took her hand and squeezed it. "You're saying he foresaw this?"

"Yes."

Fox looked over his shoulder. "How does it work?"

"I'm trying to remember. Each word is either a placeholder or a counter for something. The sentence has fifteen words. Fifteen is the number of hours, which means it's 3PM. The rabbit is one animal, so 1a. Old back then meant anybody over sixty, so that's >60. The word 'without' means you have to subtract however many words follow it, so that's -2. So the password is 3PM1a>60-2."

"You sure?" Fox asked.

"Type it in."

Fox typed the password, and an instant later, a file folder opened and revealed a video file. He clicked on it.

The video began to play. It was instantly clear that whoever had recorded the video had done so clandestinely and through a dirty glass pane. Despite that fact, Jack recognized that the large space was a warehouse of some sort. The floor was concrete, and there were large vents and lights lining the exposed unpainted ceiling. On one side of the warehouse were crates, on the other side, various machines were in different states of assembly—as if somebody was building a factory.

"That looks like an MRI machine," Ace said and pointed to the large circular equipment.

"Yeah, it looks similar, but I've never seen one that big," Lilly said. "Besides, nobody would put medical equipment in a place that's clearly not sterile. It looks dirty."

The camera panned to the left. There were shelves with amber colored glass bottles as well as IV bags, boxes with hypodermic needles and lines used for infusions. Next to the shelves there was a piece of furniture, still partially wrapped in a tarp.

"Looks like a treatment table for a clinic," Lilly commented. Then she moved her head closer to the screen. "Oh my God."

"What is it?" Jack asked.

She pointed to a spot. "I think these are restraints, as if this treatment table is meant to have somebody strapped onto it. The only time I've ever seen something like that is when I did my psych rotation."

Ace turned to Lilly. "What did they use it for?"

"Violent patients. Sometimes the orderlies had a hard time keeping patients calm when they needed to get treatment, so they would strap the patient onto the table with these leather belts, you know, like you might have seen in movies when they show an electric chair."

Jack exchanged a look with Ace and Fox. Both looked concerned. The video ended.

"Do you think this is what got Thomas killed?" Jack asked.

Ace took a breath. "We must assume that he made the recording and that it meant something to him. Enough to hide it for Lilly to find." He put his hand on Fox's shoulder. "Can you find out where the video was recorded?"

Fox nodded. "It should have the geo data embedded somewhere. If River meant for us to find this, he wouldn't have stripped the data."

It took Fox only a few keystrokes before he found the data he was looking for. "There it is, the GPS coordinates of the location." He opened a different window and pasted in the GPS data. A map opened up. In its center, a red flag pointed to the requested location.

"That's near Great Falls in Virginia, about halfway from here to Dulles International Airport," Jack said. "I think we should check it out."

"Agreed," Ace said. "You and I will go there tonight."

"I can have your back from here," Fox said.

"How?" Jack asked.

"Michelle and I can hack into a satellite and reposition it to get a visual of the area and make sure you're not running into a trap. It'll take a while, but we should get it done by tonight. There's no point in going in before it's dark and quiet anyway."

"I'm coming with you too," Lilly said and looked at Jack.

"Not a chance," Jack said. "You're safest here."

She shook her head. "You need me." She pointed to the monitor. "That's medical equipment. I'm a doctor. I'll recognize what I'm looking at. I'll be able to tell you what we're dealing with. There are clearly medications on those shelves. I need to see them close-up to figure out what they're for. It might be important."

Jack stared at her, torn between wanting to keep Lilly safe and allowing her to accompany them so she could lend her expertise.

"Damn it, Jack, Thomas was my cousin. I need to find out what he was doing there. And I can be of help."

"Fine."

He hoped he wouldn't regret this decision.

15

———————

After a hearty lunch, Jack and Lilly got a crash course about the security features of the mansion, and had a chance to get settled into the room that would be theirs for the foreseeable future. Lilly changed into clothes that Phoebe lent her, and in the late afternoon, the shoes Michelle had ordered for her online arrived.

Jack brought in the bag he'd packed for himself, which consisted of clothes as well as any items that could lead back to him should they be found, such as a few photos and some electronics, as well as his weapons. The house which he'd considered his safe house for the better part of the last three years was now devoid of any personal effects.

He'd also brought a box filled with things he used to disguise himself: wigs, beards, glasses, and hats, as well as stage make-up. The room Phoebe had prepared for them was large and comfortable, had its own bathroom, and a large closet to store the few things they had brought.

While Lilly took a nap to prepare for the long night ahead and catch up on the lost sleep of the previous night, Jack spent the afternoon in the kitchen, where he cleaned his guns. He was used to managing with little sleep. Besides, over the last three years he'd always slept with one eye open, never fully relaxing.

Fox and Michelle were busy hacking into a satellite control system, while Ace joined Jack in the kitchen.

"How long have you been together with Lilly?" Ace asked, pouring himself a large cup of coffee.

"We met seven years ago at a BBQ at Will Reed's house, Thomas's father," Jack said.

"That's not answering my question."

He should have known that Ace couldn't be fooled by the careful wording of Jack's answer. After all, they'd trained together at the Farm. Jack looked straight at his fellow Stargate agent.

"You're still sharp," Jack said.

"Have to be, or I would be dead." Ace took a sip from his coffee. "Let me guess: you hooked up only a few days ago."

"Almost true. We had a thing seven years ago. I broke it off when I joined Sheppard's program. You're aware of his conditions."

Ace nodded. "Cut all ties. He thought it would be safer for all of us. As much as I loved my father, he was wrong, though his heart was in the right place."

"He was looking out for all of us. If he hadn't been able to send us a telepathic message when they came for him, we'd all be dead now."

"Wish I knew how he did that. I've never been able to communicate telepathically with any of the other precognitives. Have you?"

Jack shook his head. "Nope. I can only assume that because he'd had his gift for a lot longer than any of us, he learned a few things that might still be in our future. Or the fact that he knew all of us personally made it easier for him to channel his gift in some way."

"We might never find out. We've gotta work with what we have." Ace paused for a moment. "Fox told me you also get the doomsday premonition."

"Is that what we call it now?" He let out a bitter laugh. "Guess it's as good a label as any. I had it again last night. It's becoming more frequent."

"As if the event is coming closer?"

"Yep. That's my guess too."

"What do you see?"

"The White House. I'm staring right at it, and then I hear an explosion behind me, feel the shockwave. It's massive." He tipped his chin up toward Ace. "How about you?"

"I'm running toward a building, but I can't reach it. I see six marines carrying a coffin from the cargo hold of a plane. An American flag is draped over it. Then there's an explosion, but like you, I can't tell where. I feel the heat and the shockwave from the explosion."

"So you don't know where you are?"

Ace shook his head. "No, but my best guess is that it has to be near a military airport."

"Joint Base Andrews is the closest to D.C.," Jack said. "Because if I feel the shockwave looking at the White House, and you feel the shockwave at a military airport, it has to be close."

"I agree. But then I'm not sure how Fox's premonition ties in with it."

"What does he see?"

"He's on the terrace of a large house by a lake. He sees the sailboats. Somebody hands him a tall glass of iced tea, and he's thirsty, but when he drinks, he feels paralyzed. He's trying to do something on the computer to stop a clock counting backward. But he can't do it. Then he feels the shockwave, and it lifts the boats out right off the water."

"Hmm. There isn't really a large lake anywhere close to Washington D.C. What if it's not a lake, but a broad river?"

For a short moment, Ace contemplated the idea. "It's possible. There are sailboats on the Potomac, and it gets quite broad in some areas."

"That's right. Fox could have seen a river, not a lake. It would tie in with what I'm seeing: that whatever impending doom the premonition is warning us of is centered in Washington D.C."

"I've had some theories about that too," Ace said. "We know that our mysterious Mr. Smith tried to force Michelle into finding Fox as he was hacking into the CIA's servers."

Jack nodded. Michelle and Fox had told him about it only ten days earlier. "Yeah, what about it?"

"I believe Smith is part of the CIA. That's how he knows about the top-secret Stargate program. Even though my father ran the program off book, there's still a possibility that somebody in his orbit got wind of it. And for whatever reason, Smith killed him or had him killed. And then he started coming after the rest of us. The program must have presented a threat to him and whatever he's planning."

"So you think he's a mole in the CIA? Working for a foreign government?"

Ace shrugged. "Possibly, but not necessarily. He could simply represent a domestic threat to the US Government. No foreign country needs to be involved in that. There are plenty of people in the US—Americans—who would like to overthrow democracy."

"Somebody has to have pretty deep pockets to finance something like that," Jack mused.

"And connections in the right places."

"So you think Smith is a bigshot in the CIA?"

"It's something we need to consider. I'm having Fox work on getting background info on anybody in the CIA who's got a high enough position with enough power and access we believe Smith to have. Michelle knows his voice, but it's not an easy job. There isn't a lot of public information about who's working for the CIA, apart from the director, and Michelle has already ruled him out. His voice is distinctly different from Smith's."

"So how is Fox finding other CIA operatives?"

"He's setting up a system to capture license plate numbers of all cars going in and out of Langley, and then tracing them back to their owners."

"Fuck, that must be thousands of cars."

"I didn't say it will be easy. That's why I'm hoping that we'll find something tonight at that warehouse that will lead us to Smith faster."

"You and me both."

16

———

When Ace, Jack, and Lilly arrived at the warehouse from Thomas's video recording, it was pitch-black. Lilly couldn't even see any streetlights. Fox's surveillance had confirmed that nobody had entered or exited the building for the last four hours—the entire time since Fox had established satellite surveillance.

"It looks deserted," Lilly said when Ace stopped the SUV.

"Seems like it," Jack agreed, "but it could be a trap."

Ace nodded from the driver's seat. "Check your comms."

Lilly touched the earpiece Ace had given her before they'd left the mansion. Ace and Jack had the same kind of earpiece.

"Fox, this is Ace," Ace said into the small microphone extending from the earpiece.

"This is Fox."

"Fox, this is Yankee."

"Yankee, all clear."

"Fox this is Lilly," Lilly said. "I should have picked a cool code name."

Lilly heard Fox's chuckle in her ear. "Lilly, you're all clear. Good luck, guys. I'll be watching from here. If I see anybody approach the building, I'll give you the signal to abort."

"Roger that," Ace said.

They exited the SUV. Lilly felt sluggish with the weight of the Kevlar vest that Ace had given her, and Jack had insisted on her wearing. Neither Jack nor Ace were wearing one. According to Ace, it was the only vest he possessed, though he was planning on getting more of them now that their group had increased in size.

Lilly was nervous, though she tried not to show it. She held a gun in her hand that she hoped she didn't have to use. Jack had given her a brief lesson in handling a gun, but she knew she was woefully inexperienced and had no idea if she would freeze when presented with a situation where she had to fire it.

Ace and Jack were equally armed. Both carried Glocks, and according to Jack, they were both expert marksmen.

She found comfort in that thought.

Together, they silently approached the building. There were windows on the side that faced the street, but they were too high up, and prevented them from looking into the building's interior. As they walked to the large door that appeared to be the main entrance, Lilly stayed behind Jack. When they stopped next to it, she peeked past Jack and saw that Ace had pulled out a listening device from the bag slung across his torso. He put a finger over his lips, cautioning them to remain silent, and placed the device against the door and leaned in, listening.

A moment later, he removed it, and whispered, "Not a sound inside, not even that of any machines."

"Okay, I'll deal with the lock. Cover me," Jack said and pulled out some tools before he started working the lock.

"All clear from the skies," Fox said into their ears. "Still no activity."

"Got it," Jack said and stepped away from the door. Then he turned to Lilly. "Stay back until we give the all clear."

She nodded.

Then she watched them as they covered each other, their guns drawn, before Ace opened the door, and Jack rushed inside. Ace followed, and a moment later, she heard Jack whisper in his microphone, "All clear. Nobody here."

Surprised at how quickly Jack and Ace had been able to determine that nobody was inside the large building, she peeked inside. Ace and Jack held flashlights in their hands and Lilly followed the beams of light.

The place was empty, not just devoid of people, but completely empty. Not a single piece of equipment, not even any trash was left in the warehouse.

Whatever had been here at the time Thomas had made the recording, it was gone now.

"Shit," Jack cursed.

"Looks like we're too late," Ace added.

Lilly pulled out her own flashlight and began to shine it along the walls and floor.

"It's a bust," Jack said and turned around.

But Lilly couldn't give up. She knew what it meant to move a lab or a medical facility. She'd done it once before when Delta Labs had outgrown their earlier facility, and knew that no move ever went without a hitch.

"They must have left something," she said, and moved her flashlight yard by yard in a square pattern. "You can't move all that equipment and those supplies without something breaking or falling."

"It's empty," Ace said, "let's go."

"Let's look around some more, just in case," Jack said with a reassuring look at Lilly.

Just then, something on the floor reflected the beam of her flashlight. "There."

She rushed to it and crouched down.

Jack and Ace were by her side in an instant, both shining their flashlights on the shiny item that was less than half an inch square.

"What is that?" she asked.

"Looks almost like an insect," Ace mused.

"It's a microdrone," Jack said. "I've read about them. They're being used to administer micro-toxins."

Lilly shot him a look. "You mean to poison people, like the Kremlin does to their political opponents?"

"Exactly," Jack said.

"If it was used to administer a toxin, there might still be traces on it. I can test for it," Lilly said.

"Let's bag it," Ace agreed and pulled a box of ammunition from his bag and emptied the ammo into the bag. "This'll have to do."

"Careful," Lilly warned, "don't get stung."

Ace used a tissue to scoop the microdrone into the little box and closed it.

"Let's get outta here," Jack said.

"Wait," Lilly said and looked closer at the spot where the microdrone had been. The dust underneath it looked to be darker than its surroundings. "Something was spilled here. It's dry now, but maybe I can analyze it to see what it was." She looked up at Jack and Ace. "Do either of you have a piece of plastic and something I can scoop this up with?"

Jack dug into his pockets, while Ace started rifling through his bag.

"Will a chewing gum wrapper do?" Jack asked.

"It'll have to," she said and took the chewing gum stick from him, unwrapped it, and then carefully scooped the dark dust onto the foil, using Jack's knife. Then she wrapped it securely and put it into the ammo box.

On the way to the SUV, Jack touched Lilly's arm and she looked at him.

"Well spotted," he praised her.

"See? It's good to have me around."

He grinned. "In more ways than one."

His words made her pulse tick up a bit. They were a good team, not just when it came to sex. And Jack had proven tonight that he valued her input.

17

───────

When they arrived back at the mansion, Fox was waiting for them with news. He ushered them into the computer room. Jack was eager to hear what he'd found.

"So, after you guys told me that the warehouse was empty," Fox began and pointed to the large monitor on the wall which depicted a graph, "I looked into the building to see who owned it. I didn't get far. The owner was clearly a shell corporation."

"Sucks," Jack said.

"Yeah, but then I thought all that equipment in there would have used a lot of energy, so I hacked into the servers of Dominion Virginia Power, which provides electricity to that area. And look at this." He pointed to the wall.

"What are we looking at?" Ace asked.

"This graph represents the monthly power usage of that warehouse over the last six months. Pretty high, particularly in the month of Thomas's death. And then two months later, the usage drops to zero."

"They moved out," Jack concluded.

"Exactly. But here's the interesting thing," Fox said and used the mouse to show a different view. "This is the daily usage for the month when Thomas died."

All thirty bars looked to be of similar height except for two. One was about double the height, the next one more than quadruple.

"What happened there?" Lilly asked.

"A huge power spike, and if we can believe the date of death on Thomas's death certificate, then the spikes occurred the day before he died and the day of his death."

Jack stared at the graph, then back at Fox. "You think Thomas was there on the days the power spiked?"

"It's possible," Fox said.

Lilly pointed to the screen. "Can you also see on which day the power usage dropped to zero?"

Fox shot her an approving look. "So we can see when they moved out? Yep." He switched to the next screen. "There it is. They disconnected all the equipment on the 28th of last month. We have to assume that they moved the equipment the same day or the next."

Jack let out a breath. This was good information. "Now all we need is to check all traffic cameras in the area to see where they moved the equipment to."

Ace nodded. "They would have needed at least a couple of moving trucks twenty-five feet long. What do you think, guys?"

"Probably, though they could have used several smaller ones, might be a little less conspicuous," Fox replied.

"I didn't see a lot of traffic cameras in the area around the warehouse," Jack said, and he'd looked, just like he always did. It had become second nature in the past three years.

"I know," Fox said. "That might make it a little harder since we won't have any footage from the point of origin and will have to rely on cameras farther away from the warehouse. It will get us a few false positives, which will take a while for us to weed through. But with five of us looking through video footage, we have a better chance."

Fox glanced at Ace. "Phoebe went to bed. She was feeling a little lightheaded."

Immediately, Ace looked concerned. "I've gotta—"

"Don't worry," Fox said. "Michelle checked on her. Turns out she didn't eat enough today, and her blood sugar was low. So Michelle made her a snack."

"I can check on her," Lilly said, "though it's been a while since I dealt with patients."

Michelle entered the room. "She's doing fine. With everything going on today, she's just a little stressed."

Jack wasn't surprised. What woman wouldn't be stressed in her situation, knowing she would bring a child into this world very soon, while her child's father was being hunted by an unknown adversary?

"Thanks, Michelle," Ace said. Then he looked at Lilly. "While we're going through the footage, can you start analyzing whether there's a chemical residue in the microdrone you found? What do you need for it?"

"My lab at Delta Labs," Lilly said.

"Can't we just get you some chemicals, and you can do the analysis here? I know a guy who can get us whatever you need in a couple of hours," Ace said.

"It's not that easy," Lilly said, shaking her head. "Since I have no idea what substance the microdrone carried, if there even is a residue, I'll have to use highly sensitive equipment to run over a hundred tests. That's not something you can pull together with a home chemistry set. Sorry. If we're lucky, it'll only take three or four hours, and I'll be out of there before people show up for work."

"It's too dangerous," Jack said immediately.

"How are you gonna get into the lab?" Ace asked.

"Access card."

"Isn't there a security guard on duty?"

"Yes, but he naps a lot."

"That doesn't guarantee that he won't see you," Jack interrupted. "He might be aware that you disappeared after the shooting in the plaza, and will ask questions, or worse, tell somebody. Nobody can know where you are."

"I get that," Lilly said, clearly trying to pacify him. "But I'll use the delivery entrance in the back. I can get to my lab without him seeing me. Trust me."

Jack held Lilly's gaze. He weighed up the risk of Lilly being seen with the benefit of finding out what substance was in the microdrone. "Fine. Under two conditions."

"Which are?"

"I'm coming with you, and you'll keep wearing the Kevlar vest."

"Oh come on, that thing is heavy," she complained.

He glared at her. "The vest stays on. I mean it."

She huffed. "Fine."

"Take one of the sedans in the garage. It's less conspicuous than your van," Ace suggested.

A few minutes later, they were on their way.

In the car, Jack saw Lilly looking at him from the side.

"Are you always this bossy?" she asked.

"I'm not bossy. I'm protecting you. You're my responsibility."

"*Macho* much?"

He tossed her a look. "Poking the sleeping bear much?"

"Touché." Then she chuckled to herself.

"What?"

"I think we're cut from the same cloth."

He smirked. "Trust me, your *cloth* is much prettier."

"We're not talking about temperament anymore, are we?"

"Thomas was right. You *are* quite direct. I like that."

"Are you trying to tell me that you like me?"

"Lilly," he said, "we've already established that I like you."

But did Lilly feel the same for him that he felt for her? Did she reciprocate the feelings he'd had even before they'd met seven years earlier? He had no right to ask this question. Lilly had no other choice but to stick with him right now.

When they reached the office park, where Delta Labs was

located, Jack switched off the headlights. There was no traffic, and he didn't want the security guard to see a car approach the building. He parked half a block away from the building, turning the car in the direction they would need to flee should something go wrong. He didn't lock the car, knowing that every second counted during an escape. Perhaps he was paranoid, but paranoid had kept him alive for the past three years.

Under his jacket in a shoulder holster, he carried his Glock. And strapped to his ankle beneath his khaki pants, was a knife.

"Lead the way," Jack said to Lilly.

"To the right there," she said, pointing to a spot on the west wall of the building.

As they approached, Jack looked around. There was a light over an unassuming door.

"Is there a camera covering that door?"

Lilly met his gaze. "Yes, but the security guard in the lobby is probably napping."

"Probably isn't good enough."

Jack pulled his Glock from its holster, then reached into his other pocket to take out the silencer he'd brought.

"Oh my God, are you gonna kill the security guard? He's an innocent guy. You can't just—"

"Of course not," he interrupted while screwing the silencer onto the muzzle of his gun. "I would never shoot an innocent." He pointed to the back door. "I need to take out the camera, so we can't be seen entering."

He aimed and pulled the trigger. The bullet hit the camera in its center, and there was barely a sound. The security guard in the front of the building wouldn't have heard it.

"Wow, you're a great shot," Lilly said.

He acknowledged her compliment with a nod. Arrived at the door, Lilly pulled out her access card and held it over the card reader. A green light flashed, and there was a beep. Lilly opened the door, and together they entered the building.

They were in a well-lit corridor.

"Are the lights on all night?" Jack whispered to Lilly.

"In the corridors, yes, but not in the offices and labs." She pointed to a door with the word *Stairs* on it. "We can't use the elevators. The guard would hear us."

Jack nodded, and they hurried into the stairwell. "Which floor?"

"Third," she replied.

Jack glanced around, but he couldn't see any cameras in the stairwell. They ascended quickly. On the third floor, Lilly led them through another well-lit corridor, then used her access card again to open a door leading into a lab. They entered the dark room and closed the door behind them.

"Don't switch on the overhead lights," Jack warned. "Take your flashlight."

Lilly switched on a flashlight and led him to a corner in the large laboratory. There she stopped and pointed to a long counter with medical equipment. Above it were hanging cabinets. "There are under-cabinet lights. I'll need to switch them on."

Jack looked toward the windows. They were far enough away from them, with sufficient pieces of furniture between them and the windows, so the light in this corner wouldn't travel far.

"Okay."

The under-cabinet lights illuminated the counter and the supplies and equipment sufficiently for Lilly to commence her work. Jack took a seat on a chair next to her, his gun with the silencer on his lap, and watched her as she went to work.

18

———

It was nearing four a.m. when Lilly had finally managed to analyze what substance had been in the microdrone.

"It's Midazolam," she said, looking at Jack.

"A poison?"

"It's a powerful sedative. It can paralyze people, and in high doses cause respiratory arrest. It's used in anesthesia. But considering the size of the microdrone, only a tiny amount could have been injected."

"Enough to knock somebody out even if just for a short while?" Jack asked.

"Yes, somebody like my size would have most likely been knocked out for a short time, but not somebody like you, although you would still have been affected and felt woozy."

"Which means if Thomas got this small amount of Midazolam, his reaction would have been impaired."

She nodded.

"That's how they might have gotten the drop on him," Jack said.

Lilly shuddered at the thought of it. Thomas would have been conscious and perhaps known what was coming. What had they done to him to warrant the usage of Midazolam?

"If they were able to get close enough with the drone to inject him with Midazolam, then wouldn't they also have been close enough to shoot him?"

Jack met her gaze. "You're right."

"Perhaps this wasn't used on him."

"Or perhaps they didn't want to kill him, not immediately anyway."

"What are you saying?" She stared at him, but he didn't immediately answer. She saw it in his face, saw what he suspected. "You think they kept him alive to torture him to give them information?"

"I'm sorry, but yes, it's very likely."

Lilly pushed back the rising tears and turned back to the counter. She was still running tests to find out what had soaked the ground beneath the microdrone. She knew it wasn't Midazolam that had leaked there. "I still need to figure out what's in this sample."

She suddenly felt Jack's hand on her shoulder. "I know that you loved him like a brother. We'll get justice for him, I promise you."

"Okay," she said with a sob.

When he tried to put his arms around her, she freed herself from them. "Don't, Jack, or I'm gonna start crying for real." She sniffled. "And I have to finish this."

"Okay," he said gently. "I wish I could help you with this, but I'm not a brain surgeon. I don't know much when it comes to—"

"Oh my God. Why haven't I thought of that?" she suddenly said and grabbed the glass slide with a tiny sample of the dust from the warehouse.

"Thought of what?"

She placed the slide underneath the microscope and looked into it. "I was so focused on it being a toxin or some other chemical. I didn't even consider..." She turned the nob on the microscope to sharpen the image. There it was.

She looked up. "It's cerebrospinal fluid."

"Cerebro—... you mean brain fluid?" Jack asked, stunned.

"Yes, the fluid that flows in and around the hollow spaces of the brain and spinal cord, and between two of the meninges..."

"Can you test that for DNA?"

"Theoretically, yes, but I don't have that kind of equipment, and"—she glanced at the clock on the counter—"there's no time anyway."

"Then let's pack up," Jack said.

It took fifteen minutes for them to return everything to its proper place, so that nobody would realize that anybody had been in the lab. Lilly switched off the under-cabinet light and turned to Jack, when she suddenly heard a sound: a beep as if somebody was using an access card to enter the laboratory.

She grabbed Jack by the sleeve of his jacket and ushered him to the end of the counter, and together they crouched down behind it. Just in time, because the door opened, and somebody flipped the light switch for the overhead lights.

Lilly held her breath, and Jack did the same. They exchanged a look, and Lilly noticed that Jack held his gun, the silencer still attached, ready to shoot. Her heart beat frantically.

She heard heavy footsteps, then the door to a cabinet was being opened. She recognized it by the sound. She lifted her palm toward Jack to tell him to stay back and risked a look past the counter. And then she saw him: the security guard was literally raiding the lab's cookie jar. He stood with his back to her, busy stuffing cookies and chocolate into the pocket of his jacket.

Lilly eased back behind the counter and gave Jack a reassuring look. He seemed to understand. Another few seconds, and the security guard closed the cupboard and walked back to the door. The door was opened once more, then he turned the light off, and left the room.

Lilly let out a breath and looked at Jack. "No wonder he's so fat. And the cookie jar is always half empty," she whispered.

Lilly was about to get up, when Jack pulled her back. "Wait. Give him a minute or two to get back to his post."

Then he put his hand on her nape and pulled her head closer to his. His lips were on hers before she could react. He kissed her hard and deep, before his kiss turned more tender. A moment later, she felt cool air brush against her lips.

"What was that for?" she asked breathlessly.

"Didn't wanna waste a perfectly good occasion for a kiss." He helped her up. "Now let's get outta here."

They didn't encounter anybody as they left the laboratory and made their way back down the same stairs they'd taken earlier. When they entered the corridor that led to the back entrance, they didn't hear any sounds. It appeared that the security guard was back at his post in the lobby, probably on a sugar high from the cookies and chocolate.

Relieved that she'd managed to get the tests done before the early birds showed up at around six a.m., Lilly turned toward the door. Jack pressed the handle down and opened it, first a sliver, peeking out, then wider.

Jack stepped outside, Lilly on his heels. There was a chill in the air. She glanced in the direction, where Jack had parked the car, turning her head slightly, when something blinded her.

"Down!" Jack cried out and pushed her down just before a bullet embedded itself in the door they'd exited five seconds earlier.

On the ground, behind a low hedge that provided a small greenbelt around the building and hid some of the utilities, Lilly crouched next to Jack.

"Same shooter?" Lilly asked breathlessly, her heart hammering in her chest.

"Not sure. It's not a rifle this time. More like a pistol with a silencer. Stay down as low as you can. I'm gonna go after him."

Lilly gripped his arm. "Are you crazy? He's gonna kill you."

"Not if I kill him first." He moved his hand along the ground and felt the pebbles that covered the soil around the hedge. He picked up one the size of an egg and handed it to Lilly. "Do me a favor. Count to five Mississippis, then toss this to your ten o'clock.

As soon as you hear the pebble hit the ground, crawl along behind this hedge until you reach the corner of the building. Stay there, and I'll come and get you."

She nodded, understanding. Nevertheless, she was shaking. "Be careful," she whispered.

"Start counting."

19

———

Jack took a second to assess the situation. This was what he'd trained for both in the military and at the Farm. He'd been in situations like this many times before, on foreign soil. And he'd always prevailed.

There were no cars in the parking lot, but there were several vans with the Delta Labs logo. In addition, there were trees and bushes, a few benches meant for employees to rest on during their breaks, trashcans, as well as a few sculptures besides the one that had been destroyed by the assassin's bullet. These objects would have to do for cover so he could outflank the shooter and get behind him.

Had the shooter taken up a position in the parking garage like on the day he'd first tried to kill Lilly, Jack and Lilly's only chance would have been to get back into the building, where they would have been trapped. But tonight, the shooter was hiding somewhere closer, and not using a rifle with a scope, but a pistol with a silencer. Clearly, he didn't want to attract any attention. And one other thing was evident: the assassin had somehow found out that Lilly would show up at her lab tonight. Jack suspected that this meant that Smith and his associates had hacked into Delta Labs security system to see if Lilly would use her access card.

The moment Jack heard the pebble hit the ground he was already behind the first Delta Labs van. He heard a second muffled shot. It was aimed in his general direction, not in Lilly's. That's why he'd had her throw the stone, to direct the shooter in his direction. And the second shot had also given him a good indication where the shooter was hiding.

Jack peered past the van and estimated the distance between his current hiding spot and his next cover. His Glock in his right hand, he took a quick breath, then sprinted out from behind the safety of the van. He saw movement, the light of a streetlamp reflecting off something and took a chance: he fired in the shooter's direction, not really expecting to hit him, but at least to make him retreat for a second or two.

Breathing hard, Jack reached a tree with a wide enough trunk behind which to seek shelter. But he couldn't stay here. There was no guarantee that the shooter wouldn't discover the ruse and figure out where Lilly was hiding. He couldn't allow that. He had to get to him first.

Using every cover available to him, Jack made a half circle to get behind the shooter's position. When he heard a sound, but couldn't determine what it was, he realized that the shooter had moved too. Closer to where Lilly was hiding.

Fuck!

Staying low, Jack moved as fast as he could without making any unnecessary noise to get closer to the assassin. He was almost there, in fact he could already hear him breathe, when Jack realized that a dim light was suddenly illuminating his arm and gun. A cloud had moved a bit to reveal the moon.

Jack dove behind a tree, just as a bullet whizzed through the air, missing him by a hair. Relying on his instinct, Jack aimed and shot into the darkness. He heard a cry of pain, and knew he'd at least wounded the guy. Not wanting to miss this opportunity, Jack charged out from behind the tree and rushed toward the assassin. He saw the muzzle of his gun glint in the faint moonlight. It was aimed at him. Jack fired.

The gun clattered to the ground, and Jack knew his bullet had found its target.

A groan came from behind the bench where the assassin had been hiding. Jack hurried toward it, his gun pointed. The moment he reached the bench, he saw the assassin lying on the ground. A foot away was the gun. Jack kicked it away, before looking at the assassin.

To his surprise, it was a woman. A black woman dressed in dark clothes. A gurgling sound came from her. She was hit in the shoulder and bleeding profusely, but it wasn't the cause of the gurgling sound. She had a second gunshot wound: a direct hit in her right chest. Judging by the amount of blood and her labored breathing, Jack realized that her lungs were filling with blood, and soon, she'd drown in it. Already now, every breath was labored.

"Lilly?" Jack called out toward the building.

"Are you okay?" she asked in return.

"Yes. I've got the shooter."

He heard the rustling of bushes, then footsteps, and a moment later Lilly reached him. Her gaze roamed over him, then she looked at the wounded assassin. She crouched down next to Jack, and a gasp came from her throat.

"Deja?" She shook her head in disbelief.

The assassin's eyes moved, and she looked at Lilly.

"You know her?" Jack asked.

"That's Deja Lashae, Uncle Will's home healthcare worker."

The revelation was shocking. And Jack knew immediately what this meant. He moved closer to Deja and put his hand on her shoulder. "Smith sent you to work for Will Reed so you could spy for him, and find Thomas?"

Deja blinked. "I had no... choice..."

He ignored the excuse. People always had a choice. Perhaps not a good one, but a choice nevertheless.

"Where's Smith?"

She breathed heavily. "Don't know..."

Jack pressed his thumb into the gunshot wound on her shoulder. Deja howled in pain, tears in her eyes.

"Smith forced me..."

"And?" Jack prompted. "Did you kill Thomas?"

Deja moved her eyes from left to right in lieu of shaking her head. "I told Smith when... when he came to see... his father... in secret." Her words were punctuated with bouts of labored breathing. "So Smith could... get him."

"So Smith killed him after you told him where he was?"

Deja's eyes drifted closed.

Jack shook her by the shoulder. "Deja, stay with me. How and where did Smith kill Thomas?"

Deja's eyes opened. "... didn't want him dead."

"What? Who didn't want him dead?"

"Smith... he needed him alive."

"But Thomas is dead," Lilly interjected and leaned over Deja. "Deja, what happened to Thomas?"

Deja turned her eyes to Lilly. "I'm sorry... Smith needed him for..."

"For what?" Lilly urged her on.

"... brain. His gift... wanted to scan it... use it..."

"Smith wanted to scan Thomas's brain?" Jack asked Deja, then looked at Lilly. "The MRI machine?"

Lilly nodded.

"Not MRI..." Deja said. "...bigger... more dangerous... the machine... it takes everything from the brain... but it's too much... takes too long... it fries... fries the brain..."

Lilly put a hand over her mouth, visibly choking down her tears. "Oh my God, Thomas... no."

"Deja, where is that equipment now? Where did Smith move it to?" Jack asked.

"Another place..." Then she looked back at Lilly. "I'm sorry... I had to protect my son... Smith knew because..."

Deja stopped moving. There was no breath. Jack checked for a pulse but found none.

"She's gone."

"What now?" Lilly stared at him, her eyes wide, anxiety rolling off her.

Jack glanced around. The sun would be up soon, and shortly after that the first employees of Delta Labs would show up for work. "There's no time to move her. We have to leave her here."

"But somebody will find her. What if they tie her death back to you or me?"

"They won't. Not if we clean up." He pulled a flashlight from his jacket pocket. "Take this and look around for the shell casings and the bullets that missed their target. Three shell casings from my gun, three from hers, and four bullets, the other two are in her." He pointed to the spots in the parking lot where his casings would have fallen, then to the spot where Deja had hidden earlier. "Pick them up."

She nodded and took the flashlight. "And what are you gonna do?"

"Dig the bullets out of her," he said.

Lilly blanched. "Are you serious?"

"Has to be done. We can't afford ballistics to trace back to this gun."

Lilly nodded, then started looking for the shell casings. Jack pulled out his knife and started digging for the bullets. The bullet in the shoulder was no problem, the one in the lungs took a little longer to dig out. By the time he was done, Lilly was back with the casings and the bullets.

"Found all six and the four bullets?"

"Yes."

"Good." He picked up Deja's gun and rifled through her pockets. He found what he was looking for: a cell phone, keys and a wallet with an ID. He stuffed the latter two items into his jacket, then took Deja's right thumb and pressed it on the cell phone until it unlocked. Quickly, he changed the PIN, so he could unlock it again at a later time. He pocketed it and rose. "Let's go."

They sped away from the scene moments later. Jack's clothes were full of Deja's blood. He dialed Ace's number and put it on speaker.

Despite the time, Ace picked up instantly. "Yes?"

"We ran into some trouble. We had to leave a dead body in Delta Labs' parking lot."

"Are you and Lilly okay?"

"Yes."

"Did you clean up?"

"Got the shell casings, bullets, the assailant's gun and her keys and ID."

"Her?"

"Yep. Tell you about it later. We've got her blood on us. Do you have a—"

"There's a room in the back of the garage. It has a high-powered shower. Take everything off and shower. I'll leave towels and fresh clothes in the closet there for both of you. Toss your clothes in the bucket next to the closet. I'll incinerate them later."

"And the guns?"

"There are plastic containers in the closet. Put them in there and bring them inside. We'll clean them later."

"All right."

"I'll see you when you get here." Ace disconnected the call.

Jack cast a quick glance at Lilly. She sat there, completely rigid. She turned her face to him. "She betrayed him."

Jack nodded. And he now understood the meaning of Will Reed's words when he'd visited him at the assisted living facility.

They're here in my house... I should have known... I told him not to come. She lied to me. It was her. The government sent her.

Will Reed had realized—too late—that Deja Lashae had been a plant by Thomas's enemies.

20

———

It was six o'clock in the morning when Lilly entered the guestroom that Phoebe had prepared for them. She and Jack had showered and changed in the room behind the garage, but the shower had been rather cold and the pressure too strong for her liking. She had understood the necessity of it and accepted it. However, the shower had made her feel like she was on a caffeine high when she knew she needed to relax and sleep.

Jack was still downstairs, filling Ace in on what the lab tests had revealed and what had transpired with Deja Lashae when they'd left the lab. Lilly shuddered when she recollected the sight of Deja bleeding out before her eyes. She'd seen dead bodies before—every medical student had—and she'd seen people die before, but not in such a violent way. And she hoped she'd never have to see anything like it again.

Lilly pulled the curtains shut, and undressed. Phoebe had been tremendously generous by providing several sets of clothes, and even left a bathrobe draped over the bed for her. The bathroom had everything Lilly could wish for: various soaps and shampoos, conditioners, deodorants, and lotions. Fresh toothbrushes and toothpaste lay on the vanity together with shaving gel and razors. Phoebe had thought of everything.

Lilly had never felt so welcome in a stranger's house before. Tears suddenly shot to her eyes. The second attempt on her life had shown her that there was no way she could ever go back home. She was reliant on strangers for her wellbeing now. Though not all were strangers. Jack wasn't. He'd risked so much for her. His own life even. Yet, he demanded nothing in return.

Lilly turned on the water and stepped into the large shower. The warm water pearled off her skin like morning dew. Her heartrate lowered, and her breath calmed. She closed her eyes and started to relax.

The door hinges creaked, and Lilly looked over her shoulder. Jack stood there, his chest bare, but still wearing the pants Ace had left for him.

"Another shower?" he asked with a smile, while his gaze swept over her body.

"This one's more relaxing." She turned her body toward him, aware that his eyes were drinking her in. Her heart started beating faster again, but this time it wasn't as a result of stress. "Do you want to join me?"

His hands moved to the top button of his khakis. "You bet."

She watched him rid himself of his pants. When he pulled his boxer briefs down, his cock jutted out, hard and heavy, its bulbous tip pointing skyward. He opened the glass shower door and stepped inside, then pulled her to him.

"Are you okay?" he asked. "I know what happened earlier must have scared you."

"It did. But you were there, and you saved me. That's the second time now." She looked up at him and slid her hand onto his nape to bring his face to hers. "Would you like me to thank you now?"

"Thank me?" He shook his head. "You being alive is thanks enough."

She slid her other hand down his torso, until it brushed against his erection.

Jack hissed in a breath.

"Does that mean you don't want me to drop to my knees right here"—she met his gaze and licked her lips—"and suck you until you come?"

Jack slid his hand onto her backside and yanked her toward him so his cock pressed into her stomach. His lips parted.

Pleased with the effect her words had on him, she added, "I seem to remember that you enjoyed that very much seven years ago."

"Goddamn it, Lilly," he murmured against her lips, "we need to get some shuteye, but with you talking like that, you're robbing me of my self-control." He rubbed his cock against her skin. He kissed her hard, but only for a few seconds, before he released her. "Now get on your knees, baby, and suck me."

At his command, a shiver went down her spine and made her nipples harden and her clit throb. With the water from the shower running down her back, Lilly dropped to her knees, her head at the same height as his groin. Jack gripped his erection by the base and brought the tip of it to Lilly's lips.

Slowly, teasingly, Lilly opened her mouth and licked over the sensitive skin of the tip, then wrapped her lips around the hard shaft and slid down on him as far as she could.

"Fuck!" Jack cursed.

She felt him sway for an instant, before he braced himself against the tile wall behind her. Lilly placed her hands on his hips and began to withdraw a little, then pulled him deeper into her mouth again.

Jack cupped her head with both hands. "Easy, baby, or I'm gonna spill in ten seconds flat."

She looked up at him and met his gaze. His eyes shone the same way as seven years earlier, with the same intensity and passion. She saw the man from back then in his new face, saw that he was still the same, still the man who had been so insatiable that night long ago that she'd slept so deeply that she hadn't heard him leave. Only this time, she saw the promise in his eyes, the promise that this time it would be different. This time he wouldn't leave.

Lilly put one hand around his root and began to suck him deep and hard. She enjoyed his masculine smell, the salty taste of his precum, the soft skin over his hard rod. Jack moved in synch with her as if they'd done this a million times. His moans bounced off the shower walls, amplifying, telling her how close he was to his climax. The closer he got, the faster her tempo became. She needed him to lose control. She needed to know that he couldn't resist her, just like she couldn't resist him, that they were equals.

"Fuck, Lilly!" he cried out and pulled himself from her mouth.

Before she realized what he was doing, she found herself pressed against the tiles, her back to Jack, his hands on her hips. He pulled them back and brought her ass to his groin. She felt his erection between her thighs. She braced herself against the wall just as Jack thrust into her. A violent shudder raced through her, and a moan ripped from her throat.

"Jack!"

He held tightly onto her hips, controlling her movements. His mouth was at her neck. "Now you'll feel what happens when you drive me to the edge of my self-control."

She would have chuckled, but Jack thrusting into her hard and deep robbed her of her breath. Her body felt as if in flames. Nothing had ever felt better than Jack's cock in her, stretching her to her limits, demanding her submission, driving her to ecstasy. He was controlling every move now, setting the tempo and the rhythm, and she let him.

Still thrusting hard, Jack released her hips and ran his hands up on both sides of her torso, then slid them to her front, cupping her breasts, and teasing her nipples with his fingers.

"You got me so randy..." He breathed hard. "... with your mouth around my cock. Next time you do that, be warned: I won't pull out."

She turned her face to the side. "I never asked you to."

The answer seemed to ratchet his arousal even higher. His tempo increased, his thrusts became harder. One hand suddenly dropped to her pussy, and with expert precision, he slid his fingers over her clitoris.

Lilly moaned, her arousal already dancing on the edge. It wouldn't take much to make her tumble over it. Jack kissed her neck, his cock plunging deep into her tight channel, his hand caressing her center of pleasure. She couldn't stop the approach of her orgasm, couldn't halt it even if her life depended on it. Her entire body shuddered with pleasure as wave after wave crested and drowned her over and over again, until she felt Jack's cock spasm and shoot his hot semen into her.

Lilly's legs were shaking, her knees threatening to buckle, when she felt Jack's arm wrap around her waist steadying her. He was still inside her, still hard.

"I've got you," he murmured in her ear.

She turned her head and offered her lips. He kissed her gently. Then his cock slipped from her as he turned her in his arms and pressed her to his chest.

"See what you do to me," Jack said softly, "you turn me into a beast."

"I like a little beast in my man."

"That's a good thing, 'cause I don't know how to turn off the beast when I'm with you."

21

———

It was midday, when Jack went to the computer room in the mansion, where Fox and Ace were hard at work. Ace sat at a computer and looked over his shoulder for a moment then continued with his work.

Fox greeted him. "Ace filled me in on what happened last night. The news is all over it."

"They won't find anything. Shame she bled out so quickly. I'm afraid I didn't get much out of her before she died."

"Well, it's something. At least we know that they are using that big MRI-type machine to scan the brain, not that I have any idea why."

Jack nodded. "And that it's so invasive that the patient dies."

Ace turned away from the computer. "We must assume that they put Thomas in that machine, and that it eventually killed him. It would make sense that they couldn't allow for his body to fall into the wrong hands, or an autopsy might have revealed what really happened."

"Yeah," Jack said, "and that means the medical examiner whom they got to sign his death certificate had to be eliminated too. No loose ends. Did you guys find anything on Deja Lashae? Who was she really?"

Ace pointed to the computer. "She was in the military until she gave birth to a son. No father in the picture. She worked private security after that."

Jack looked over his shoulder into the screen where Deja's military record was displayed.

"That's why she knew her way around a gun. Did she have sniper training?"

"Yes." Ace scrolled farther down.

"So she was the assassin from earlier?" Jack asked.

Fox stood up and joined them. "Confirmed. Her cell phone pinged off a nearby cell tower around the same time as she tried to kill Lilly in the plaza in front of Delta Labs. Guess her private security jobs included assassinations."

For a moment, Jack thought about what Deja had said before her death. "I don't think so. She mentioned that she wanted to protect her son. Maybe Smith had something on him?"

"Let's see," Fox said and nudged Ace aside, before he started tapping away on the keyboard. A few moments later, he pointed to the screen. "There it is. Her son, Kobe Lashae, is in the military and has been accused of sexually assaulting a female soldier in his unit. He's facing a court-martial. Apparently, there were no witnesses. It's her word against his."

"Twenty bucks says the charges are false," Jack said. "Smith fabricated them so he could force Deja to do his bidding, first by spying on Will Reed to find out where Thomas was, and then by using her sniper skills to kill Lilly when she was asking too many questions."

"Looks that way," Fox said. "We might find something similar in Dr. Amy Price's background. Smith used her to cover up how Thomas died."

Jack grunted. "For all we know, the ashes they sent to his father weren't even his." He ran a hand through his hair. "You said you guys checked Deja's cell phone. Anything else on it that might help us?"

Fox switched screens. A map of Washington D.C. and parts of Virginia and Maryland appeared. Lots of dots were sprinkled over it. "These are all the places where Deja's phone pinged off various cell towers."

"She got around," Jack said. "That's not gonna help much."

Ace pointed to a spot on the map. "That's where we found the microdrone in the warehouse. Deja was in that same area around the time of Thomas's death."

"Which is around the time of the power surge I mentioned yesterday," Fox interjected.

Ace nodded. "So we think Deja's story checks out. She might have handed Thomas over to Smith, or at the very least, disclosed his location to Smith so he could capture him."

Jack shook his head. "There's one thing that doesn't quite fit with this scenario."

"What do you mean?"

"Thomas found the warehouse and not only had time to make a recording, but also hide that recording at his father's house. And Will Reed said that *they* were in his house, and that *she* lied to him, that it was *her*, and that the government sent *her*. I think either Thomas or his father found out that Deja was working for Smith. Maybe Thomas was able to track her movements to that warehouse, and that's how he was able to record what was inside. Perhaps he tried to take Deja down later at Will Reed's house, but Smith or Deja had already deployed the microdrone so they could get the drop on him."

Fox and Ace exchanged a look.

"Hmm, that's possible," Ace said. "Still doesn't tell us where they've set up shop now."

"You found no vans in the area that might have transported the equipment?" Jack asked.

"Too many," Fox said. "We can't possibly follow all of them." Then he smiled unexpectedly. "So Michelle and I are working on searching the power grid for any power surges and cross reference them with any sightings of large vans that might have delivered the scanning equipment."

"That's smart. Anything yet?" Jack asked.

"We only got the program up and running in the last half hour. It's not plug and play, it takes some finessing."

Ace chuckled. "I think this is the part where Fox is looking for an acknowledgement of his superior IT skills."

Fox simply rolled his eyes. "I'll let you guys know when we find something. It can take a few hours."

"We can't just sit around and twiddle our thumbs in the meantime," Jack said.

Ace cast him a look. "Then let's get all our gear ready so we're prepared when we get a location. Since we have no idea how often they move their facility, we might only get a short window of opportunity."

"Yeah, that's what worries me too," Jack agreed. He hated sitting around doing nothing.

Jack followed Ace out of the computer room. They crossed the foyer, and Jack heard voices coming from the kitchen. Lilly was talking to Michelle and Phoebe.

"I haven't thanked you yet for taking us in," Jack said, while Ace opened a door, and Jack followed him down the stairs into the basement.

"You're welcome. Tell you the truth, Phoebe likes the company. She was a reporter, you know, and used to be around a lot of people on a daily basis. Now it's just me and her, and Fox and Michelle, but they're normally not here all day and night."

The basement was a massive room divided into several sections. Overhead fluorescent lights illuminated the space which was lined with large cupboards. It also housed a workbench, a large sink, and various machines.

"We have everything to make Molotov cocktails, pipe bombs, smoke bombs, and whatever else your heart desires."

Jack gave an appreciative nod. "Totally beats my setup."

"Let's get to work."

22

———

Lilly set the large table in the kitchen for a late lunch. She'd helped Phoebe with preparing sandwiches and a salad, while Michelle had gone to help Fox in the computer room. She'd sounded confident that they would soon be able to pin down a location of where Smith had set up the new facility after abandoning the warehouse in Great Falls, Virginia.

On a small TV mounted on the wall, a news program reported about the dead body found in the office park. They hadn't been able to identify Deja yet, but Lilly knew that it would be only a matter of time, even though Jack had taken her wallet, phone, and keys.

"... according to police sources," a reporter standing in front of Delta Labs said.

Lilly heard steps at the door and looked over her shoulder to see Ace and Jack enter.

The news reporter continued, "However, after the shooting on Wednesday at the same location, employees in this office park, which houses several pharmaceutical companies and laboratories, raise the question whether these attacks are aimed at the companies and their pricing practices, rather than at a specific person."

"That's a lucky twist," Jack said, pointing to the TV.

"Nothing to do with luck," Ace replied. "Phoebe still has contacts in the media. She dropped a hint to turn the investigation into a different direction."

Jack walked up to Lilly and kissed her on the cheek. "You okay?"

"I will be." As long as she didn't dwell too long on all the things that could have happened had Jack not been able to take Deja out. "You guys must be famished."

Phoebe entered the kitchen. Ace put an arm around her and kissed her, then put his hand on her stomach, and they exchanged a tender look.

Lilly turned away and caught Jack looking at her. His gaze was just as loving as the look Ace and Phoebe had exchanged. Her heart fluttered, and she felt heat rush to her cheeks.

"Food, great!" Fox said from the door, as he and Michelle entered. He headed for the table and sat down. "I'm famished." He loaded his plate with salad and a sandwich.

"I need a bite too," Jack admitted and walked toward the table.

Lilly followed him, but before Jack reached the table, he suddenly stopped, and she almost bumped into him.

"Jack?"

He didn't reply, merely stood there. Lilly walked around him, and gripped his forearm, when she noticed that he stared straight ahead, his chest heaving now.

"What's wrong?"

"Shit," Fox let out and rose. "Let go of him!"

Lilly instantly took her hand off Jack's arm, stunned by Fox's sharp words.

"He's having a premonition. Don't pull him out of it," Ace warned. "He needs to see it through the end."

Surprised and at the same time curious, Lilly looked at Jack. His face twitched and his eyes moved as if he was reacting to something. She had never thought about what it would be like to see him have a premonition. When he'd had a nightmarish vision during his sleep, she'd shaken him to come out of it, and now she wondered whether she shouldn't have done it. Perhaps he would have seen more, had she not tried to wake him.

All of a sudden, Jack swayed, and it looked like he would fall forward, but Ace had already gripped him to steady him.

"Thanks, thanks," Jack said breathlessly.

Nobody said a word. Clearly, Ace and Fox knew that he needed a few seconds to find his bearings.

"I'm good," Jack said, then straightened his shoulders. "But we've got a problem."

"What did you see?" Ace asked.

"The big MRI machine, the one in Thomas's video. If Deja was right when she said it would fry somebody's brain, then we have no time to lose. I saw them strapping a guy into it. They were starting the scan. At five p.m."

Lilly's gaze shot to the clock on the wall. "That leaves us only three hours…"

"And there's something else," Jack added with a look at Ace and Fox. "I've seen the guy before. Black, mid-thirties, shaved head, fit. I think he's one of us."

"Fuck," Ace hissed and charged to the computer room, Jack on his heels.

Fox snatched his sandwich, took a big bite, and hurried after them. Lilly followed them, not hungry anymore. She hadn't been able to save Thomas, but if she could do anything to help save the next poor soul from suffering irreversible brain damage at the hands of this Mr. Smith, she would do it.

Michelle and Phoebe joined Lilly as she hurried after the men.

"All-hands-on-deck," Michelle said.

In the computer room, Ace had already pulled up a file with photos and names and was projecting it onto the big monitor on the wall.

"What is that?" Lilly asked Phoebe who stood next to her.

"A list of all Stargate agents," she murmured.

Lilly watched as Ace scrolled through the photos, while Jack fixated on the monitor. She recognized several of the men: Fox, Ace, Thomas, and Jack—the old Jack, the way he'd looked before the plastic surgery.

"Stop!" Jack ordered and pointed to the monitor. "That's him, that's the man they'll strap into that machine."

"Jay Garner, Code Name Tiger," Ace read. "Okay, everybody, we've got very little time. Phoebe and Lilly, get the van assault-ready."

"Assault-ready?" Lilly echoed.

"Phoebe will show you. Michelle and Fox, find a way to speed up the process of cross-referencing any power surges with the routes of vans large enough to have moved the equipment; Jack, you and I will do manual cross-checks of everything the computer spits out from the searches. Let's do this. Clock's ticking."

23

——————

Half an hour after he'd had the premonition of Tiger's brain being scanned, Jack stared at a dot on the map.

"You sure that's the place?" Jack asked, looking at Fox and Michelle.

"Positive," Fox said. "Shortly after Thomas's death several vans drove onto the street where this building is located. Unfortunately, there are no cameras that would show that the vans entered the building and unloaded their cargo."

Fox pointed to the video taken by a traffic camera at an intersection. "An hour later, the same vans are coming back." He pointed to the next recording. "Do you see this?"

Jack focused on the vans and their wheels. "Can you zoom in on the wheels?"

Fox did as asked.

Fox was correct. And Jack could see it now too. "They unloaded their cargo. On the way there, the vans were heavier. These are lighter... You can see more of the wheels."

Fox nodded. "Exactly. There are very few buildings on this street. And the only building that had increased electricity use in the last month is this one." Fox switched to Google Street View and zoomed in on a large warehouse. "It coincides with the delivery of the equipment. And earlier today, their electricity usage increased even more. Not quite to the spike we saw at the previous location though."

"They're ramping up," Ace interjected. "It's as if they're doing a dry run before..."

He didn't need to finish his sentence. Everybody in the room knew what he meant.

Jack nodded. "They could be calibrating the machine so it's ready for tonight. We've gotta hurry."

Ace looked at Michelle. "Do you still have control over the satellite from yesterday?"

"Sure do. It's gonna take less than five minutes to reposition it to cover this building," Michelle said. "And once set up, I can monitor it remotely."

"Why remotely?" Jack asked.

"Because I'm coming with you."

"Too dangerous," Jack said and looked to Fox, surprised that he hadn't already protested.

But Fox just lifted his shoulders in surrender. "Don't look at me, man. Michelle makes her own decisions, no matter what my objections are."

Jack saw Phoebe and Lilly enter.

"I'm more useful if I come with you guys," Michelle added. "I'm the only one who's ever heard Smith's voice. If he's there, I'll recognize him. It's our chance to catch him."

"She's got a point," Ace said. "But we only have one Kevlar vest."

"Actually, we have more than one," Phoebe said. "Van's ready by the way." Then she looked at the large monitor on the wall. "Is that the place?"

Ace nodded. "Yep. What did you mean by saying we have more than one Kevlar vest?"

Phoebe motioned to Michelle. "Michelle ordered some after you guys went to the warehouse in Great Falls."

Jack, Ace, and Fox stared at Michelle.

Michelle smirked. "Turns out you can buy Kevlar vests on Amazon." She shrugged. "With next- day delivery. They arrived just before lunch."

"You had them delivered here?" Jack asked, incredulous. "They can track—"

"I'm not at idiot, Yankee," Michelle interrupted. "I used an account I've never used before and had them delivered to a house a few blocks away. The family who lives there is on vacation. Phoebe picked up the package earlier today."

She walked to one of the computers, and sat down, her fingers already hovering over the keyboard.

Phoebe grinned. "At least I get to do something useful occasionally. I left them in the garage."

Jack exchanged a look with Fox and Ace. "Okay, then, let's hit the road as soon as Michelle is done with the satellite repositioning."

"I'm coming with you too," Lilly said.

Jack whipped his head toward her. "No, not happening."

"But you just heard Michelle. There are plenty of Kevlar vests for everybody. And you're letting Michelle come."

Jack ground his teeth. "That's not my decision. It's Michelle and Fox's."

"And this is mine," Lilly said firmly. "I'm a doctor, and Tiger may need medical assistance. You have no idea what condition he's in."

"And what makes you think you do?" Jack growled. "You said yourself not too long ago, that it's been years since you dealt with patients."

"That doesn't mean that I can't detect what symptoms someone has and what they mean. We might not have a lot of time to help Tiger. Or are you gonna drive him to the hospital once you free him?"

Jack remained silent, as did his fellow Stargate agents. He knew full well that going to a hospital to seek treatment meant exposing themselves to their enemies.

"Well, that's what I thought," Lilly said after a few seconds of silence.

"We'll bring him back here," Jack said, even though he knew he'd already lost this battle with Lilly. She was no pushover, but then, had he really expected to win this argument?

"Not good enough. I'm coming with you."

Ace and Fox suddenly exchanged a look and chuckled.

"You're not gonna back me up, are you?" Jack asked them. When they shook their heads, Jack looked at Lilly. "You'll stay outside the building, until I ask you to come inside. Is that clear?"

Lilly nodded. "Crystal."

"Okay," Ace said, taking charge. "Let's roll."

24

The facility Smith had transferred the machinery to after abandoning the one in Great Falls was located in a wooded area outside of Manassas, Virginia. The drive should only have taken an hour and fifteen minutes, but an accident on the freeway resulted in a long delay. The detour they'd been forced to take had added almost another hour to their trip. By the time they arrived at their destination, it was fifteen minutes to five.

Ace had been driving, with Jack riding shotgun. Michelle, who sat in the back of the van with Fox, Lilly, and a laptop, had been keeping them apprised of what was going on in the vicinity of the building. Everybody in the car was wearing a Kevlar vest and was equipped with earpieces so that they could communicate easily once in the building.

"There's definitely something going on," Michelle said now as they stopped about five-hundred yards away.

Jack turned in the passenger seat and looked at Michelle. "Can you tell if they have surveillance cameras around the building?"

"It's hard to see on the satellite image, but let's assume there are cameras to warn them about anybody approaching," Michelle said.

"We need to take them out," Jack said.

"Easier said than done," Michelle said. "Problem is if I cut the power to the facility, they'll know we're coming."

"We'd better keep that in our back pocket," Ace interjected, then looked at Jack. "How good of a shot are you?"

"Good enough," Jack said, understanding what Ace was planning. "Michelle, how many entrances are we looking at?"

"One in the front, one in the back, plus the loading dock."

Michelle turned the laptop for everybody to see as she pointed out the spots on the grainy satellite image.

"We have to assume they have cameras at all three entrances. If we can get a clear shot at them, taking all cameras out at the same time, they might think that it's just a technical glitch," Jack mused.

"Okay," Ace said, "we can do that. We'll have to use the silencers and approach on foot through the woods."

"Let's do it," Jack agreed. "Fox?"

Fox pulled out his gun and screwed the silencer onto the muzzle. "I'm ready when you are."

"Lilly, you and Michelle stay here until we know what's going on inside," Jack said.

"Be careful," Lilly said. She looked worried.

"I'm always careful," Jack assured her.

Moments later, Ace, Fox, and Jack exited the vehicle.

"Fox, you take the back entrance, I'll take the front," Ace said, "Yankee, you'll take the loading dock."

They fanned out and marched into the woods. The trees and brush provided good cover. Smith and his cronies had probably chosen this location because the building couldn't easily be seen from the street, thus hiding their nefarious activities from the public. But the hidden location also meant that Jack and his fellow Stargate agents could get close to the building without being seen.

Jack hurried through the woods, constantly scanning the area for any trip wires or cameras. He didn't detect any. If he were to set up a facility like this, he'd make sure to spread motion sensors amidst the trees around the building to be warned about an ambush.

Jack was almost in place, when he heard Ace in his ear. "I have a visual of the camera over the front entrance."

"Getting closer," Fox said.

"Almost there," Jack added.

He was approximately a hundred yards from the building now, and as he snuck past a large tree, he spotted the loading dock. A white van was parked there, but the driver's cabin was empty. Jack let his eyes roam, but he couldn't see anybody. He had to assume that the driver was inside the building.

The double doors leading from the loading dock into the building were in Jack's sight, though he had to aim at the camera above it from the side, since the van blocked his direct view.

"In position," Jack whispered into his microphone.

"Same," Fox said.

"On my count of three," Ace said. "One, two, three."

Jack squeezed the trigger. The bullet found its target. The camera lens shattered, and the glass fragments fell on the ground. "Direct hit."

"Front door camera is destroyed."

"Back door too," Fox added.

"Approach your ingress points," Ace said. "Report when you've cracked the lock."

Keeping as low as possible, and using everything at his disposal for cover, Jack approached the loading dock. He glanced around but saw nobody. The windows on this side of the building were high up, and he was pretty sure that nobody was looking through them. If his premonition was correct, they were too busy inside. He glanced at his watch. Five minutes to five p.m. They were cutting it close, too close for his liking.

When Jack reached the double doors at the loading dock, he realized that they were ajar.

"Loading dock doors are not locked," he reported to Ace.

"Working on the back door," Fox said.

"I need a few seconds at the front," Ace replied.

Jack pressed himself against the wall next to the double doors, his eyes scanning his surroundings. Seconds felt like minutes.

"Ace?"

"Got it," Ace said.

"Me too," Fox replied.

"See you inside," Ace said.

Jack eased the door open and listened for sounds from inside, then peeked into the interior. The loading dock area was dimly lit and quiet. Jack squeezed inside. He found himself in an area with pallets and packing materials, empty crates and boxes. A curtain of thick plastic sheets, which were common in refrigerated spaces like those of a meat-packing plant, separated the area from the rest of the building. It dulled the voices and sounds coming from the main part of the building.

Jack parted the plastic sheets by an inch and peered into the space. It didn't take him long to assess what they were dealing with. He slid the plastic shut again and retreated a few yards, before he dared whisper into his mic.

"Loading dock is clear. The machine is in the southeast quadrant. Don't have a clear view. There are pallets stacked in the northwest quadrant, partially blocking my view."

"I've got a direct view," Fox confirmed. "Tiger is already in the machine."

"I hear the sound. The machine is running," Ace added. "Fox, how many men do you see?"

"Three close to the machine. Two are wearing white coats, one of them is injecting something in Tiger's IV drip. A third guy is wearing blue overalls."

"I see the one in the blue overalls," Ace said. "Yankee?"

Jack peeked into the room once more. "Negative, can't see any of them from my vantage point." Then he picked up a movement in the corner of his eye and whipped his head. "Two people approaching from the northeast quadrant. One in a suit. The other dressed in black. He's armed."

The armed man moved his head in Jack's direction, and Jack quickly jerked back behind the thick plastic curtain.

"The suit and the armed guy are in my view," Ace said a moment later.

"There's another armed guy, he's coming from another door," Fox said. "Perhaps a bathroom."

"Where's he going?" Jack asked.

"Heading in your direction, Yankee."

Jack stepped to the side to press himself against the wall next to the plastic curtain, his gun ready, when he heard Michelle's voice in his ear.

"Somebody is heading for the loading dock."

Jack couldn't answer to ask for more details, because the armed man just parted the plastic curtain to the area where Jack was waiting. He didn't step through, instead, he looked toward the double doors.

"Can anybody hear me?" Michelle asked.

Ace and Fox didn't answer either, which could only mean that they too were too close to Smith's henchmen and had to remain silent.

Jack shifted his weight from one foot to the other to turn his torso, so he could aim at the armed man and take him out. Debris under his foot made a sound. It wasn't loud, but sufficient for the guard to turn his head and reach for his gun.

"Security breach!" the guy yelled.

Jack spun to aim his gun in his direction, trying not to offer the guy too broad a target. Jack shot, but the guy did too, and his opponent's gunshot echoed in the small space. Jack felt the bullet graze his arm but didn't feel any pain. Blood spurted from the guard's biceps, but he was still standing.

Jack fired a second shot, before the assailant could aim with his injured arm. The second bullet hit him squarely in the chest. From the corner of his eye, Jack saw a movement coming from the double doors. Too late he turned. The man Michelle had warned him about had already reached him and tackled him to the ground, knocking the wind out of him.

Jack heard shouting from inside the facility where the MRI machine was located. He had to assume that everybody had heard the guard's gunshot, and that Ace and Fox did their best to stop more of them coming toward the loading dock.

Jack punched his attacker and noticed only now that he'd lost his gun during the fall. Luckily, the other guy didn't have a gun either, or, Jack assumed, he wouldn't have charged him like a football player but shot him instead. The assailant was heavier than Jack by at least forty pounds. Despite this advantage and his position on the ground, Jack was able to hold him off.

"Michelle, cut the power!"

It was Ace's voice he heard through the earpiece.

"On it!" came Michelle's reply.

Meanwhile Jack managed to land a punch in the assailant's throat, making him choke. He used the temporary distraction to kick him off and roll to the side. Jack jumped up and saw his gun a few feet from where the armed guard had fallen. Next to the dead guy lay a gun, too. Jack rushed to his Glock. The assailant staggered to his feet, his eyes on the dead man's gun, just as the lights went out.

Michelle had managed to cut the power. Only a sliver of light shone from the partially closed double doors into the space where Jack was fighting. Jack lunged for his gun, hoping that he'd estimated the distance correctly. With the fingertips of his left hand, Jack felt the cold metal of the Glock. He stretched farther to wrap his hand around it.

Just then, he heard a loud humming sound like that of a furnace, and an instant later, the lights were back on. Jack had no time to transfer his gun into his right hand, because the assailant now had a gun pointed in his direction. Jack pulled the trigger twice in quick succession. The heavy opponent fell like a dead tree.

"Michelle, the damn power is back on!" Fox yelled.

"They've got backup generators. I've gotta come in," Michelle replied, breathing hard as if she was already running toward the building.

Jack jumped up, heading through the plastic curtain. More gunshots came from the area where the oversized MRI machine was located. Simultaneously, he heard through his earpiece how somebody cried out in pain. He didn't know whether it was Fox or Ace, but he knew his friends were in trouble.

25

Lilly raced toward the building alongside Michelle.

"Jack is gonna be furious," Michelle warned.

"Yeah, well, I'm gonna deal with that later. Right now, we have to help him and the others."

She'd heard the shots from inside the facility, and knew they'd come from their enemies, because they were too loud to come from guns with silencers.

"I have to find the backup generator," Michelle said. "Help me with the search on the outside of the building."

"I can't," Lilly said, "I have to get Tiger out of the machine, or he'll suffer permanent brain damage."

Arriving at the front entrance, Michelle let out a harsh breath. "Be careful. Or Jack will have my head too."

"Find the generator. Go!" Lilly said and opened the unlocked front door.

Inside, she looked around. She'd heard the men talk about quadrants and their various directions on their comms, but northwest and southeast meant nothing to her. Couldn't they just have said front left or back right? No, they had to use cardinal points, as if she knew her way around a compass!

Pallets stacked up high blocked her view to the back of the building. Letting her eyes roam to her left and right, Lilly made her way to the left edge of the pallets, where a path led deeper into the interior of the building. At the corner, she peered past the pallets. She saw the top of the MRI machine behind a forklift truck and a few metal shelving units. From behind them, there were grunts and other sounds indicating that several men were involved in hand-to-hand combat, though she couldn't see much. Glass and metal items shattered, and again there was a gunshot. She caught a glimpse of Jack being thrown against a metal rack, and a man dressed in black diving after him.

Shit! She had to help Jack and the others, even though she knew she had no chance if one of the bad guys was coming after her. But with Ace, Fox, and Jack fighting their opponents, she was the only one who could disconnect Tiger from the machine.

Lilly ran down the narrow path between the stacks of pallets, staying low so that nobody would see her approach.

"Ace, on your left!" she heard Jack's voice in her earpiece.

Hearing Jack's voice meant he was gaining the upper hand on his opponent. But she had no time to look for him or Ace or Fox to see if they were doing okay. She headed straight for the MRI machine. She could see it clearly now. In front of it, a man in a white coat lay on the ground, bleeding profusely from a chest wound.

On the gurney lay a black man. She couldn't see his face since his upper body was inside the machine. He was dressed in green scrubs, and barefoot. His wrists, feet, and waist were chained to the gurney with leather straps. Lilly had to assume that his head and shoulders were equally restrained. On the top of his left hand was an IV port, which was connected to a drip hanging from an IV pole.

Next to the MRI machine was a console, a server tower, and two computer monitors that looked like they were recording brain waves, as well as another panel with buttons. She had to assume that this was the electronic equipment which controlled the machine. She cast a look to her left and saw Fox fighting with a man in blue overalls, tossing him against a door. Behind Fox another guy lunged for him.

"Fox, behind you!" she yelled into her microphone.

She saw Fox whirling around on his heel, but the guy was already grabbing him.

"Lilly?" Jack said through the earpiece, sounding winded. "Get the fuck out!"

"I've gotta get Tiger out of the machine," she said and turned back to the control panel. She placed her gun on the table, while she searched frantically for an off switch, but there was none. There were several buttons with symbols on them.

Fuck! She hated guessing. She took a breath. Four buttons had arrows. She pressed one of them and looked at the gurney. It moved farther into the machine.

"Crap!"

She pressed the button with the arrow pointing in the other direction. The gurney moved in the opposite direction. Lilly breathed a sigh of relief as she saw Tiger's chest, and finally his head coming out, while the MRI machine was still droning on and continuing its circular motion. Tiger's head was locked in a brace. It almost looked like a helmet, though it was made of plastic. She rushed to his side.

"Tiger, I'm here to get you out," she said quickly and examined the locking mechanism.

A look at his face told her that he was semi-conscious.

"Stay with me, Tiger," she said softly. "Stay awake."

She tried to turn the helmet, so she could figure out how it was attached, and had to realize that the helmet was part of the gurney, and she couldn't see any clasps or anything else to figure out how to open it so she could free Tiger from it.

Fuck!

Maybe if she took all the other restraints off him first, she would be able to move him sufficiently to find an opening mechanism. Quickly, she undid the leather restraints on his feet, waist, and wrists.

"Tiger, wiggle your hands and feet if you can hear me," she said.

Behind her, she heard a stack of pallets crash, and men cry out in pain, but she had no time to look at what was going on. She had to get Tiger off the gurney, though she realized that he wouldn't be able to assist her in any way: his hands and feet weren't moving. He was paralyzed, most likely from the drugs they'd given him. She looked at the tray next to the console. A vial and a needle lay on it. Midazolam, just as she'd suspected. She yanked the drip from Tiger's IV port but kept the port in his hand. Most likely the drip was just a saline solution, but she couldn't be sure that it didn't contain more of the sedative to keep him paralyzed.

"Listen to my voice, Tiger, stay with me," she said.

Lilly had some difficulty loosening the leather strap that was tightly bound across Tiger's pectorals and biceps. She had to yank on it, using all her strength to unhook him from it. Her heart beat frantically not only from the physical stress, but also the mental one. She cast a quick look to where the Stargate agents were fighting.

She saw Ace running after a man in a white coat as he tried to flee through the back exit. Fox was still fighting his opponent, trying to wrestle the gun from him. She didn't have a clear view of Jack and the man he fought with. Their confrontation had taken them behind the pallets.

Lilly turned back to the console, looking for anything that would indicate how she could get Tiger's head out of the tight helmet. Maybe one of the buttons with a symbol on it? She felt sweat collect on her nape and forehead but forced herself to remain calm. She had to keep her wits about her if she wanted to help Tiger.

A movement to her right made her snap her head in its direction. Too late. The middle-aged man in the business suit was pointing a gun at her. She froze.

"Step away from the console," he ordered and made a shooing motion with his gun.

Her gun lay on the console, where she'd placed it earlier to free her hands. The man saw it too.

"I said step away from the console, Miss Davis, and not a word out of your mouth, or it'll be your last."

She recognized his voice then. It was the same man who'd pretended to be Henry Sheppard. This had to be Smith. She took a step back and away from the console. Why hadn't he shot her yet? She glanced toward the area where Fox battled it out with the man in the blue overalls. He wasn't looking in her direction. When she turned back to look at Smith's gun, she realized that it didn't have a silencer.

She understood then. He didn't want to shoot her, because it would alert Fox and Jack. She remained stationary, hoping that one of the Stargate agents would eventually see that she was in trouble.

Smith walked closer to the server tower, his gun still trained on her. He was only three feet from her, when he leaned toward the server, pressed a lever on it, and a compartment opened. He reached for it and pulled out a component that look like a hard drive. He shoved it in his jacket pocket. This was why he hadn't fled yet. He needed whatever data the machine had collected.

Smith leaned toward the console again and hit a button. With horror, Lilly watched as the gurney moved back into the MRI machine, Tiger still hooked to it by the helmet. And even if the mechanism gave way, he wouldn't be able to escape, the paralyzing drug still in his system.

"Lilly!" Jack screamed from somewhere behind her, his voice echoing in her earpiece at the same time. Jack had seen the situation she was in. He'd get her out of it and help her save Tiger.

Her relief was short-lived. Smith grabbed her, and in the process her earpiece fell to the ground. He pulled her in front of him, one arm around her torso, imprisoning her arms, the other hand pointing his gun underneath her chin, its muzzle pressing against the soft flesh underneath her jaw.

She was his hostage and his human shield now.

26

———————

This was his worst nightmare playing out in front of him. Jack had dispatched his opponent into the beyond and rushed toward the MRI machine to help free Tiger, calling out to Lilly, before he'd seen the man with the gun behind her.

The way the man in the suit held the gun to Lilly's head meant that even an experienced marksman like Jack couldn't take Lilly's captor out before he killed Lilly.

"Drop your weapon on the floor," the man ordered.

Jack hesitated, but he had no choice. He bent down and laid the Glock on the ground, before standing up again.

"Now kick it in my direction."

Jack did as he was told, never taking his eyes off him and Lilly. Lilly's face was a mask of fear, and he wished he could tell her that everything would be alright.

"Let her go," Jack demanded.

A chuckle came from the man. "Not gonna happen. She's my ticket out of here."

"What do you want?"

The man ignored the question, and instead looked past Jack. Footsteps were approaching.

"Fox," the man said, "drop your gun and kick it to your left, or I'll blow Lilly's head off."

"You won't do that," Fox said. "You need Lilly alive to get out of here. It's hard using a dead body as a shield."

"Fox!" Jack warned. "Do as he says. He's holding a gun right under her chin."

The last sentence wasn't for Fox's benefit but for Ace's and Michelle's. They would hear him via their earpieces. However, no reply came from either one. Had Ace not defeated his opponent? Was he injured, or worse, dead?

"Listen to your friend, Fox," Lilly's captor said, and began to slowly walk backwards, dragging Lilly with him, using her as a shield so Fox wouldn't get a clear shot. "I'm getting very impatient. And when I get impatient, I do irrational things." He jerked the muzzle of his gun upward, driving it deeper into the soft area under Lilly's chin.

Lilly cried out in pain. Jack saw her eyes fill with tears. Hopelessness spread in them.

"Fine," Fox finally capitulated.

Jack heard him put the gun on the ground then kick it away.

"Well, was that so hard?" Lilly's captor said sarcastically. "Now, if you don't mind, I've got places to go, people to see..."

He walked sideways with Lilly still in his clutches, heading for the front exit.

Through his earpiece, Jack suddenly heard Michelle whisper, "Lights out in three."

Jack glanced at the spot where his gun had landed, while counting in his head.

One.

Two.

The lights went out in the entire building, and the MRI machine finally shut down.

In the darkness, Jack lunged for his gun. Meanwhile, he heard shuffling, cursing, and grunting, and a cry of pain coming from Lilly.

Lilly's captor was trying to get away with her as his hostage. Jack searched the floor for his gun, but it took him several seconds to find it. Finally, he gripped the handle and rushed toward the opposite wall. He heard somebody crashing into a stack of pallets, the sound indicating that a stack was collapsing.

"Got the gun," Jack whispered into the microphone.

"Me too," Fox replied in the same way.

"Fox, cover me," Jack said.

"Roger that," Fox replied.

"Michelle, lights on in three," Jack ordered.

Again, Jack counted in his head.

The lights came on, and at the same time, the MRI machine started humming again.

Jack stared in the direction that Lilly's captor had taken and saw the stack of pallets that had collapsed. Next to it, Lilly lay, groaning. Jack raced to her.

"Lilly, are you alright? Oh my God, are you shot?"

He reached her and crouched down, letting his eyes roam over her body.

"No, he slammed me against the pallets when the lights went out," Lilly said, wincing as he helped her up. She breathed hard.

"Are you sure you're okay?"

"I'm fine." She pointed to the front exit. "I recognized his voice. He was the one pretending to be Henry Sheppard."

"Then that must be Smith," Jack guessed.

Fox was already running past them. "Let's get Smith."

"I need your help getting Tiger out of the machine," Lilly said, already running toward it. "His head is stuck in a helmet attached to the gurney."

"Shit!" Jack cursed, following Lilly.

Via his microphone he said, "Ace, where are you? Michelle, do you have a visual of Ace? Smith is escaping through the front."

After a few seconds, Michelle finally replied, "Ace is okay. Got knocked out, but he's alright."

"I'm okay," Ace said with a groan.

"Fox is heading out the front, following Smith. I need to help Lilly get Tiger out of the MRI machine." Jack reached the machine.

"I can cut the power again," Michelle said.

"Yes, cut the power," Jack said.

"No!" Lilly cried out. "I need the power to get the gurney out. Or Tiger will be stuck inside."

"Did you hear that, Michelle? Leave the power on."

"Okay."

Jack watched as Lilly pressed a button, and slowly the gurney with Tiger on it came out of the machine, until Tiger's entire body was outside. Jack instantly saw why Lilly needed his help. The helmet around Tiger's head was fused with the gurney, and the gurney in turn was firmly attached to the machine. There was no way detaching the gurney and transporting Tiger with it out of the machine. They had to free him from the helmet now.

"Can you get the helmet off him?" Lilly asked frantically, while she rifled through the supplies of syringes and bottles on the shelf next to the machine.

"I'll take care of it," Jack said, then glanced at Lilly as she filled a syringe with a clear liquid from a medicine bottle. "What are you doing?"

"Tiger got drugged with Midazolam. I'm giving him Flumazenil to counteract the Midazolam."

Jack took a closer look at the helmet and how it was closed around Tiger's head. At first it looked like the white plastic was one solid piece, but then he sensed a groove with his fingers. He pressed against it, and suddenly the helmet parted in the front, and its two halves opened up like a clamshell.

"I've got it."

He saw how Lilly injected the syringe into Tiger's IV port, then set the empty syringe aside. She leaned over Tiger's head. His eyes were open.

"You're okay, Tiger, I gave you an antidote. I know you can't move yet, but the paralysis is only temporary. I promise you, you'll be fine."

It looked like Tiger tried to blink, but the movement of his eyelids was barely visible.

"Tiger, I'm Yankee. You're safe now."

Jack looked over his shoulder when he heard footsteps rapidly approaching. He saw Fox, Ace, and Michelle coming toward him.

"Did you get Smith?" Jack asked.

Ace and Fox both shook their heads.

"He took off before we could get to him," Fox said.

"Sorry, I wasn't much help. That jerk I fought with had a mean right hook," Ace said, rubbing his jaw. Then he pointed to the gurney. "How's Tiger? Is he gonna make it?"

"Yes," Lilly said. "He'll be fine. But you'll have to carry him out of here. It'll be a couple of hours before the paralysis wears off."

Ace nodded. "Okay, then let's rig this place first. Fox, can you set up the charges, while Yankee and I bring all the bodies in here?"

Fox nodded.

"Did anybody else escape?" Jack asked.

Ace shook his head. "Only Smith."

"We'll worry about him later," Jack said. "Let's clean up, so we can get outta here."

27

———

After removing all guns from the facility in Manassas and rigging it with explosives, Michelle, Lilly, Jack, and his fellow Stargate agents Ace, Fox, and Tiger, left to return to Ace's mansion. Michelle captured the explosion via the hijacked satellite, and downloaded it to her tablet, before erasing everything the satellite had captured while redirecting and repositioning it to its original location. Both Fox and Michelle assured them that nobody would find any footage of what had happened at Smith's secret facility.

It took several hours, until Tiger was well enough to sit up and tell them what had happened to him, and even more importantly, why Smith had captured him and tried to scan his brain.

Phoebe had prepared the large living room in the mansion, setting out food and drinks for the team to recover from their mission, while Lilly checked everybody for injuries and administered first aid.

Luckily, everybody had gotten away with only bruises. The bullet that had grazed Jack's arm had done no real damage, apart from taking off a layer of skin. Ace's face was swollen from the punches he'd sustained from his opponent, and Lilly had assured

Phoebe that her fiancé showed no signs of a concussion. Finally, Lilly could breathe a sigh of relief. It was a wonder that they'd all survived without being gravely injured. While she was still concerned about Tiger's health, and wished she could send him to get checked out at a hospital, Lilly knew that it wasn't an option.

Lilly put the impressive first-aid kit that Phoebe had given her aside. By the looks of it, it was an often-used item. She planned to expand the kit just as soon as she was able to lay her hands on other medical supplies and medications such as antibiotics and antidotes for common drugs. After the experience earlier, she had the feeling that this wouldn't be the last time that she had to apply the things she'd learned during her rotation in the emergency room.

Lilly took a seat next to Jack on the couch. Everybody was waiting patiently, yet eagerly, to hear what Tiger, whose real name was Jay Garner, had learned during his capture.

He now wore clothes Ace had given him, a pair of khakis and a T-shirt. He looked better. His light grey eyes looked clear now, an indication that the drugs in his system had mostly been eliminated. His head was shorn bald, and on it, electrodes had left impressions. They would soon disappear. By all accounts, physically, Tiger would make a full recovery. When it came to his mental and emotional state, they could only wait and see.

"Thank you," Tiger said now, "if you all hadn't come to get me out of there, my brain would be porridge now." He looked at all of them in turn. "I know what risks you had to take."

"Comes with the job," Jack said. "Tell us what happened. How did they get you?"

Tiger gave a one-shouldered shrug. "Like my dad always said: no good deed goes unpunished. I had a vision of a house fire in which an older woman burned to death with her two grandchildren. I got there when the fire had already cut off the exit. I smashed in a window in the back and pulled the woman and children to safety. But I didn't get away quickly enough, and some eager bystander videoed the fire instead of helping, and then posted it on his social media accounts."

"Smith must have recognized you," Jack said.

"That's what I figured, but how?" Tiger asked. "How did he have a photo of what I look like?"

"I can explain that," Fox said. "When I went to Langley to hack into Sheppard's old files to find his master file on all his Stargate agents, I noticed that somebody had erased them. I'm assuming that the person who did that was Smith, but not before he made a copy for himself."

"So he knows about all of us?"

"I'm afraid so," Fox said, "but so do we. I've got the same list."

"How? You just said Smith erased it," Tiger said, confused.

"He did, but there was a backup I was able to access. That's how we knew you were one of us." He tipped his chin toward Jack. "So when Yankee had a vision about you in that MRI machine, we knew we had to get you."

Tiger nodded, understanding. Lilly noticed that Tiger seemed to tremble all of a sudden.

"Are you okay? Do you need to lie down?" Lilly asked.

"I'm fine. Just a little shaken." He swallowed, then continued, "The machine that they put me in... it... I don't know how to describe it, but it was the worst thing I've ever felt in my entire life. Worse than getting a wisdom tooth pulled without anesthesia. My head... it was like they were trying to suck my brain out of my skull."

Now Ace leaned forward. "Do you know what they were trying to do?"

Tiger nodded. "I was conscious most of the time before they put me into the machine. But I couldn't move a muscle."

"The Midazolam, it paralyzed you," Lilly explained.

"Yes, but I could listen. I suppose they didn't care at that point how much I found out. My guess is that I wouldn't have survived the brain scan..." He looked at the assembled. Everybody looked glum. "Yeah, thought so. Anyway, they said that they were accessing that part of my brain that's responsible for the premonitions that all of us precognitives experience."

"To do what?" Jack asked.

"From what I could piece together, they're trying to build a massive quantum computer using our brain waves."

Fox and Michelle gasped.

"What does a quantum computer do?" Lilly asked the two computer geeks.

Fox and Michelle exchanged a look. Then Fox looked at Lilly, "Not sure how to explain it, but basically a quantum computer is much more advanced than any other computer, and can compute data with a speed and efficiency that'll make a regular PC look like an abacus."

Michelle nodded. "Researchers are speculating that a quantum computer might be able to predict outcomes of events that haven't happened yet..."

"...and if Smith is scanning the brains of Stargate agents," Fox continued, "to feed this data to a quantum computer, then we must assume that the computer they're building will be able to make predictions that are a hundred percent accurate."

"However, to make it accurate," Michelle said, continuing Fox's thought process, "they need a larger sample size."

Everybody knew what that meant.

"They'll have to scan as many brains of precognitives as possible," Lilly guessed.

Fox nodded. "And whoever has control of this quantum computer will have unprecedented power."

"Nobody can be allowed to wield this much power," Jack said.

"We'll have to stop them from building that computer," Ace added.

"At least you blew up the facility. You destroyed the machine," Tiger said. "That'll slow Smith down. And he's lost all the data he's collected so far."

Lilly shook her head. "Smith snatched the hard drive just before he used me as a human shield. I saw him put it in his pocket. He still has the data."

Ace nodded. "They can rebuild the machine, if they don't already have another one in reserve. Smith won't stop until he's got what he wants."

"We have to stop Smith," Jack said. "Cut off the head of the snake." He looked at Michelle. "Anything on the satellite images of where Smith was fleeing to?"

"I'm afraid not. He left in a red sedan, but he was out of the satellite's range after a few miles. Fox and I are already combing through traffic cameras in the area. Nothing so far. He probably ditched the car as soon as he could, and fled."

"If he reached a train station or metro station, he could be anywhere by now," Fox added.

"At least we know now what he looks like," Jack said.

Lilly noticed Tiger press a hand to his temple. Concerned, she addressed him, "Tiger, does your head hurt? Are you in pain? I can give you something for that."

He forced a smile. "I don't want any meds. They'll just dull my senses. There's something I'm forgetting. Something important."

"About Smith?" Jack asked eagerly.

"Yeah, something he said on the phone. He spoke to somebody." Tiger closed his eyes.

"Take deep breaths," Lilly said, trying to calm him. "In and out, just breathe."

Everybody in the living room fell silent.

"Breathe," Lilly continued. "Don't force it. It'll come to you."

Tiger took a few more breaths, then he finally opened his eyes again. "I remember now. Smith talked to somebody on the phone. He called him Mr. Jones. He reassured him that the project was on track. Judging by the way he spoke to him, I think Jones is Smith's boss. Smith isn't the big brains behind the operation."

"That changes things," Jack said. "We can't kill Smith when we find him. At least not right away. We need him to lead us to Jones."

Lilly looked at the four Stargate agents. They looked determined now. Somehow, they would find Smith and Jones, and stop their nefarious plan.

"Tomorrow, we hatch a plan," Ace said. "Get some rest tonight, all of you. We've got lots of work ahead of us."

28

A glass of whiskey in his hand, Smith paced nervously in the living room of his house, which overlooked the Potomac. Beyond it, the lights of the city twinkled, but he was in no mood to admire their beauty. He had problems that needed to be addressed. He knew he couldn't delay the call he had to make any longer, or Jones would find out from other sources that the warehouse in Manassas was no more.

By the time the Stargate agents had blown the place and all its contents to smithereens, Smith had been well on his way to safety. He'd seen the explosion from a high point several miles away. It left him without a doubt that nothing in the building could have survived.

He'd recognized two of the agents, Ace and Fox, from their photos in Henry Sheppard's old file. But he had no idea who the third man who'd helped them was. He'd also recognized Michelle Andrews, the hacker who'd once done his bidding, but who'd switched to the other camp without delivering Fox to him. He'd pretty much suspected that she'd shacked up with Fox, and that their paths would cross again.

The biggest surprise had been Lilly Davis. It irked him to no end that she was still alive. She'd caused him enough trouble by digging into River's death. The news earlier in the day that Deja Lashae had been killed before sending Lilly Davis to her maker, had pissed him off. Could nobody do their job? Did he have to do everything himself? Three assassins were dead, one killed in the pursuit of Ace, the other while trying to silence Michelle Andrews, and the third one while trying to take care of Lilly Davis. Not to speak of the seven men—four scientists and three security guards—who'd died in Manassas, although they were replaceable.

Smith emptied the glass and set it down. He pulled his cell phone from his pocket and clicked on the only contact saved on the burner. It rang twice, before the call was answered.

"What is it?"

"Mr. Jones, there's been an... incident."

There was a short pause, in which Smith only heard Jones's breathing. What mood was he in tonight? It probably didn't matter, because once Smith confessed what had happened, he'd be in a bad mood for sure.

"What happened?" Jones ground out.

Smith imagined Jones clenching his jaw while trying to maintain a pleasant facial expression so that whoever looked at him couldn't tell that he was annoyed.

"We lost the agent, Tiger."

"What the fuck? Didn't I tell you to go slow this time? Don't you learn from your mistakes? River could have lasted longer and given us more, if you hadn't been in a rush."

"We never even got a chance at tapping Tiger's brain. There was an ambush," he said, bracing for another outburst from the man he served.

"Who?"

"At least two other Stargate agents, possibly a third one, but he wasn't on Sheppard's list. And two civilians." He decided not to mention that the civilians were women. It would make him look even more incompetent in Jones's eyes.

"And your people, they couldn't handle them? Last I checked you had seven people there plus yourself!"

"They knew exactly where to attack."

"How many of our people did we lose?"

"All of them."

"Fuck! And the Stargate agents? Tell me you got at least one of them."

Smith swallowed hard. "No. There was no opportunity for it. I had to—"

"Run away with your tail tucked between your legs?" Jones asked sarcastically.

"I got the backup drives. I saved the data. We have all the data we've already collected from the precognitives. I managed to get out before the place blew up."

That seemed to pacify Jones a little bit, because his voice sounded calmer when he said, "This will delay things."

"I know, sir, but we can be up and running at a new location in a month."

There was a brief pause of silence.

"Do it."

"Thank you, sir."

"And, Smith…"

Smith held his breath.

"Don't disappoint me again. Or I'll have to replace you."

There was a click in the line signaling that Jones had hung up. Smith wiped the sweat from his brow. He poured himself another glass of whiskey. Next time he'd have to do his dirty work himself. No more contract killers. They'd been naught for three. And he couldn't afford another mistake, because Jones's threat to replace him wasn't an idle one, and it didn't mean he'd have to find a new job.

It meant a bullet in the head. That's how Jones dealt with people who became a liability.

29

Jack entered the guest room that would be his and Lilly's home for the foreseeable future and closed the door behind him. He kicked his boots off, pulled his shirt over his head and tossed it on the nearby chair. He sat down on the bed and pulled his socks off, then continued with his khakis. He noticed the bruises on his body, but they would heal quickly. What would take a little longer was the emotional toll the events at the warehouse had taken. Seeing Lilly in Smith's clutches had been more than he could handle.

Lilly appeared in the door to the bathroom, wearing only a bathrobe. When she met his gaze, a sheepish expression spread on her face.

"Hey," she said, her voice a mere whisper.

Jack stood up and walked to her, now wearing only his boxer briefs. "You and I have something to discuss."

He noticed her swallow hard.

"I know."

She lifted her hands to put them on his naked chest, but as much as he wanted to feel her touch, they had to have this conversation now. He snatched her wrists and held them captive.

"Do you have any idea what you did tonight?"

Lilly had the good sense to look ashamed. "I'm sorry, but if I hadn't come in when I did, Tiger might not have made it."

"Smith could have killed you."

"I'm still alive," she murmured.

"You're lucky to be alive," he corrected her. He inhaled a shaky breath at the recollection of the danger she'd been in. "I don't wanna go through this again. Next time, you listen—"

"Jack, please don't be mad."

He glared at her. "I almost lost you! Don't you understand? I could have lost you before I ever had the chance to tell you what you mean to me. I—"

"What I mean to you?"

His heart thundered in his ears. "Lilly, damn it, I love you."

For a moment she was silent. "Oh." Lilly's face froze.

He immediately regretted having confessed his love to her. He hadn't planned this. Hadn't wanted to burden her with this knowledge, or pressure her to reciprocate when she didn't feel the same.

"Forget it," he said quickly and released her wrists.

He turned away, but she gripped his forearm and jerked him back.

"Oh, no, Jack Porter, you don't get to retract what you just said." She shook her head. "Not a chance. You don't get to walk away and break my heart a second time. You don't get to tell me you love me, and then disappear from my life! Do you really think I would still be here with you if I didn't feel the same? If I didn't love you too? Jack, you're such an idiot. I think I'm gonna have to teach you how relationships work since clearly, you've never had one."

Jack gaped at her, his heart beating excitedly. "Are you saying—"

"—that you're a piece of work? Yes."

"Not that part," he said, smirking now. "The part about you loving me."

She smiled at him. "Oh, that part? Yes." She sighed softly. "Jack, I got to know you through all the stories Thomas told me about you, about the time you were deployed together. When I finally met you at that BBQ, I was already in love with you. That feeling never changed, even though I was so angry that you left, so disappointed that you didn't feel the same. No matter how hard I tried to forget you, I couldn't. I still love you, and with every day I love you more. You're a good man, Jack, honorable, loyal, and brave. And I don't care that we have to live in hiding, because wherever you are will be my home. You, Jack, are my home."

Lilly's fierce declaration almost brought him to his knees. He was speechless. How could two people feel the same, yet manage to suppress their true desire for so many years?

Jack pulled her into his arms. "I'll never leave you again. I promise," he murmured at her lips.

"And I promise I'll never let you go."

"I'll hold you to that."

She brushed her lips against his. "Now stop talking and make love to me."

Jack pressed his lips against hers and felt them part to invite him in. He swept his tongue into her sweet cavern and explored her, while he reached for the belt of her robe and untied it. Her bathrobe fell open, and he freed her from it, before he pulled her naked body against his. Her body molded to his, her soft skin and lush curves sliding against his firm muscles, complementing his body perfectly.

Lilly was the yin to his yang. Together they were stronger than apart. She'd proven this to him tonight, proven that she was his equal in more things than just sex. She was strong, brave, and loyal. And sexier than any woman he'd ever met. As he laid her on the bed and rid himself of his boxer briefs, he knew that he'd never get tired of her, of her body welcoming him, her pussy weeping for him.

Without inhibition, she spread her legs for him, while she held his gaze, demanding without words that he take her, that he claim what was his all along. When her eyes dropped to his erection, and she licked her lips, Jack knew that they wouldn't get much sleep tonight, even though they were both exhausted. It didn't matter. He'd trade sleep for making love to Lilly anytime.

As he braced himself over her and thrust his cock deep into her, Lilly's eyes closed, and a long moan rolled over her lips.

"Tell me again that you love me," he demanded, and slowly withdrew his cock but for the tip.

She lifted her lids. "I love you, Jack."

At her words, he plunged back into her tight pussy, harder this time.

"Tell me you're mine," he said as he withdrew again.

This time she put her hands on his hips. "I'm yours." She pulled him down on her, impaling herself on his cock. "And you're mine."

The impact robbed him of his breath, while a shudder traveled down his spine and into his balls.

"Fuck!" he let out.

There was no slowing things down now. He needed to take her hard, needed to bury himself balls-deep in her, feeling her muscles contract around him as if she wanted to imprison him.

Their bodies began to move in synch with each other, his cock descending and withdrawing in a steady rhythm, the tempo accelerating. He captured her lips, kissed her with the same passion as he drove into her sweet body, and felt his arousal reach a fever pitch. Every time they came together, he could feel the smoothness with which skin rubbed against glistening skin, perspiration making every contact feel like sliding against velvet or silk.

Every moan, every sigh they shared was further proof of the love between them. Jack knew that there would never be another woman for him, no matter if he died tomorrow or in fifty years. His heart would always belong to Lilly.

"I love you," he murmured.

Together, they climaxed. Jack felt Lilly's interior muscles spasm around him as he shot his seed into her. When their movements stilled, he looked into her eyes, and saw his own love reflected in them.

"I wish I could thank Thomas for bringing us together," Jack said.

"He knew all along that we were meant for each other," Lilly replied.

"Yes, he did." And perhaps there was a reason for it. "Perhaps, Thomas saw it in one of his premonitions..."

"We'll never know," Lilly said, "but I'll always be grateful to him."

"So will I."

ABOUT THE AUTHOR

Tina Folsom was born in Germany and has been living in English speaking countries since 1991. Tina has always been a bit of a globe trotter.

She lived in Munich, Lausanne, London, New York City, Los Angeles, San Francisco, and Sacramento. She has now made a beach town in Southern California her permanent home with her American husband and her dog.

She's written 50 romance novels in English most of which are translated into German, French, and Spanish.

https://tinawritesromance.com
tina@tinawritesromance.com

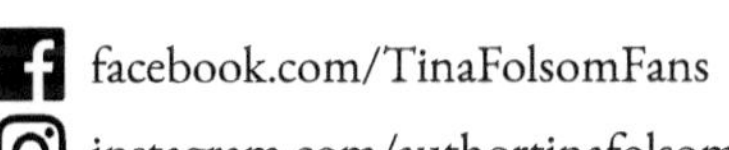

facebook.com/TinaFolsomFans
instagram.com/authortinafolsom